PENGUIN BOOKS

Madness

Roald Dahl is best known for his mischievous, wildly inventive stories for children. But throughout his life he was also a prolific and acclaimed writer of stories for adults. These sinister, surprising tales continue to entertain, amuse and shock generations of readers even today.

Madness

ROALD DAHL

PENGUIN BOOKS

PENGUIN BOOKS

UK | USA | Canada | Ireland | Australia
India | New Zealand | South Africa

Penguin Books is part of the Penguin Random House group of companies
whose addresses can be found at global.penguinrandomhouse.com.

These stories have been previously published in a variety of publications.
Details of each story's original publication are provided at the start of
each chapter and constitute an extension of this copyright page.
This collection first published in Penguin Books 2016

001

Set in 12.5/14.75pt Garamond MT Std
Typeset by Jouve (UK), Milton Keynes
Printed in Great Britain by Clays Ltd, St Ives plc

A CIP catalogue record for this book is available from the British Library

ISBN: 978-0-718-18563-3

www.greenpenguin.co.uk

MIX
Paper from
responsible sources
FSC® C018179

Penguin Random House is committed to a
sustainable future for our business, our readers
and our planet. This book is made from Forest
Stewardship Council® certified paper.

Contents

Edward the Conqueror

First published in *The New Yorker*
(31 October 1953)

Louisa, holding a dishcloth in her hand, stepped out the kitchen door at the back of the house into the cool October sunshine.

'Edward!' she called. '*Ed-ward!* Lunch is ready!'

She paused a moment, listening; then she strolled out on to the lawn and continued across it – a little shadow attending her – skirting the rose bed and touching the sundial lightly with one finger as she went by. She moved rather gracefully for a woman who was small and plump, with a lilt in her walk and a gentle swinging of the shoulders and the arms. She passed under the mulberry tree on to the brick path, then went all the way along the path until she came to the place where she could look down into the dip at the end of this large garden.

'*Edward!* Lunch!'

She could see him now, about eighty yards away, down in the dip on the edge of the wood – the tallish narrow figure in khaki slacks and dark-green sweater, working beside a big bonfire with a fork in his hands, pitching brambles on to the top of the fire. It was blazing fiercely, with orange flames and clouds of milky smoke, and the smoke was drifting back over the garden with a wonderful scent of autumn and burning leaves.

Louisa went down the slope towards her husband. Had she wanted, she could easily have called again and made herself heard, but there was something about a first-class bonfire that impelled her towards it, right up close so she could feel the heat and listen to it burn.

'Lunch,' she said, approaching.

'Oh, hello. All right – yes. I'm coming.'

'*What* a good fire.'

'I've decided to clear this place right out,' her husband said. 'I'm sick and tired of all these brambles.' His long face was wet with perspiration. There were small beads of it clinging all over his moustache like dew, and two little rivers were running down his throat on to the turtleneck of the sweater.

'You better be careful you don't overdo it, Edward.'

'Louisa, I do wish you'd stop treating me as though I were eighty. A bit of exercise never did anyone any harm.'

'Yes, dear, I know. Oh, Edward! Look! Look!'

The man turned and looked at Louisa, who was pointing now to the far side of the bonfire.

'Look, Edward! The cat!'

Sitting on the ground, so close to the fire that the flames sometimes seemed actually to be touching it, was a large cat of a most unusual colour. It stayed quite still, with its head on one side and its nose in the air, watching the man and woman with a cool yellow eye.

'It'll get burned!' Louisa cried, and she dropped the dishcloth and darted swiftly in and grabbed it with both hands, whisking it away and putting it on the grass well clear of the flames.

'You crazy cat,' she said, dusting off her hands. 'What's the matter with you?'

'Cats know what they're doing,' the husband said. 'You'll never find a cat doing something it doesn't want. Not cats.'

'Whose is it? You ever seen it before?'

'No, I never have. Damn peculiar colour.'

The cat had seated itself on the grass and was regarding them with a sidewise look. There was a veiled inward expression about the eyes, something curiously omniscient and pensive, and around the nose a most delicate air of contempt, as though the sight of these two middle-aged persons – the one small, plump and rosy, the other lean and extremely sweaty – were a matter of some surprise but very little importance. For a cat, it certainly had an unusual colour – a pure silvery grey with no blue in it at all – and the hair was very long and silky.

Louisa bent down and stroked its head. 'You must go home,' she said. 'Be a good cat now and go on home to where you belong.'

The man and wife started to stroll back up the hill towards the house. The cat got up and followed, at a distance at first, but edging closer and closer as they went along. Soon it was alongside them, then it was ahead, leading the way across the lawn to the house, and walking as though it owned the whole place, holding its tail straight up in the air, like a mast.

'Go home,' the man said. 'Go on home. We don't want you.'

But when they reached the house, it came in with them,

3

and Louisa gave it some milk in the kitchen. During lunch, it hopped up on to the spare chair between them and sat through the meal with its head just above the level of the table, watching the proceedings with those dark-yellow eyes which kept moving slowly from the woman to the man and back again.

'I don't like this cat,' Edward said.

'Oh, I think it's a beautiful cat. I do hope it stays a little while.'

'Now, listen to me, Louisa. The creature can't possibly stay here. It belongs to someone else. It's lost. And if it's still trying to hang around this afternoon, you'd better take it to the police. They'll see it gets home.'

After lunch, Edward returned to his gardening. Louisa, as usual, went to the piano. She was a competent pianist and a genuine music-lover, and almost every afternoon she spent an hour or so playing for herself. The cat was now lying on the sofa, and she paused to stroke it as she went by. It opened its eyes, looked at her a moment, then closed them again and went back to sleep.

'You're an awfully nice cat,' she said. 'And such a beautiful colour. I wish I could keep you.' Then her fingers, moving over the fur on the cat's head, came into contact with a small lump, a little growth just above the right eye.

'Poor cat,' she said. 'You've got bumps on your beautiful face. You must be getting old.'

She went over and sat down on the long piano bench, but she didn't immediately start to play. One of her special little pleasures was to make every day a kind of concert day, with a carefully arranged programme which she worked out in detail before she began. She never liked to break her enjoyment by having to stop while she wondered what to play next. All she wanted was a brief pause after each piece while the audience clapped enthusiastically and called for more. It was so much nicer to imagine an audience, and now and again while she was playing – on the lucky days, that is – the room would begin to swim and fade and darken, and she would see nothing but row upon row of seats and a sea of white faces upturned towards her, listening with a rapt and adoring concentration.

Sometimes she played from memory, sometimes from music. Today she would play from memory; that was the way she felt. And what should the programme be? She sat before the piano with her small hands clasped on her lap, a plump rosy little person with a round and still quite pretty face, her hair done up in a neat bun at the back of her head. By looking slightly to the right, she could see the cat curled up asleep on the sofa, and its silvery-grey coat was beautiful against the purple of the cushion. How about some Bach to begin with? Or, better still, Vivaldi. The Bach adaptation for organ of the D minor *Concerto Grosso*. Yes – that first. Then perhaps a little Schumann. *Carnaval*? That would be fun. And after that – well, a touch of Liszt for a change. One of the *Petrarch Sonnets*. The second one – that was the loveliest – the E major. Then another Schumann, another of his gay ones – *Kinderszenen*. And lastly, for the encore, a Brahms waltz, or maybe two of them if she felt like it.

Vivaldi, Schumann, Liszt, Schumann, Brahms. A very nice programme, one that she could play easily without the music. She moved herself a little closer to the piano and paused a moment while someone in the audience – already she could feel that this was one of the lucky days – while someone in the audience had his last cough; then, with the slow grace that accompanied nearly all her movements, she lifted her hands to the keyboard and began to play.

She wasn't, at that particular moment, watching the cat at all – as a matter of fact she had forgotten its presence – but as the first deep notes of the Vivaldi sounded softly in the room, she became aware, out of the corner of one eye, of a sudden flurry, a flash of movement on the sofa to her right. She stopped playing at once. 'What is it?' she said, turning to the cat. 'What's the matter?'

The animal, who a few seconds before had been sleeping peacefully, was now sitting bolt upright on the sofa, very tense, the whole body aquiver, ears up and eyes wide open, staring at the piano.

'Did I frighten you?' she asked gently. 'Perhaps you've never heard music before.'

No, she told herself. I don't think that's what it is. On second thoughts, it seemed to her that the cat's attitude was not one of fear. There was no shrinking or backing away. If anything, there was a leaning forward, a kind of eagerness about the creature, and the face – well, there was rather an odd expression on the face, something of a mixture between surprise and shock. Of course, the face of a cat is a small and fairly expressionless thing, but if you watch carefully the eyes and ears working together, and particularly that little area of mobile skin below the ears and slightly to one side, you can occasionally see the reflection of very powerful emotions. Louisa was watching the face closely now, and because she was curious to see what would happen a second time, she reached out her hands to the keyboard and began again to play the Vivaldi.

This time the cat was ready for it, and all that happened to begin with was a small extra tensing of the body. But as the music swelled and quickened into that first exciting rhythm of the introduction to the fugue, a strange look that amounted almost to ecstasy began to settle upon the creature's face. The ears, which up to then had been pricked up straight, were gradually drawn back, the eyelids drooped, the head went over to one side, and at that moment Louisa could have sworn that the animal was actually *appreciating* the work.

What she saw (or thought she saw) was something she had noticed many times on the faces of people listening very closely to a piece of music. When the sound takes complete hold of them and drowns them in itself, a peculiar, intensely ecstatic look comes over them that you can recognize as easily as a smile. So far as Louisa could see, the cat was now wearing almost exactly this kind of look.

Louisa finished the fugue, then played the siciliana, and all the way through she kept watching the cat on the sofa. The final proof for her that the animal was listening came at the end, when the music stopped. It blinked, stirred itself a little, stretched a leg, settled into a more comfortable position, took a quick glance round the room, then looked expectantly in her direction. It was precisely the way a concert-goer reacts when the music momentarily releases him in the pause between two movements of a symphony. The behaviour was so thoroughly human it gave her a queer agitated feeling in the chest.

'You like that?' she asked. 'You like Vivaldi?'

The moment she'd spoken, she felt ridiculous, but not – and this to her was a trifle sinister – not quite so ridiculous as she knew she should have felt.

Well, there was nothing for it now except to go straight ahead with the next number on the programme, which was *Carnaval*. As soon as she began to play, the cat again stiffened and sat up straighter; then, as it became slowly and blissfully saturated with the sound, it relapsed into that queer melting mood of ecstasy that seemed to have something to do with drowning and with dreaming. It was really an extravagant sight – quite a comical one, too – to see this silvery cat sitting on the sofa and being carried away like this. And what made it more screwy than ever, Louisa thought, was the fact that this music, which the animal seemed to be enjoying so much, was manifestly too *difficult*, too *classical*, to be appreciated by the majority of humans in the world.

Maybe, she thought, the creature's not really enjoying it at all. Maybe it's a sort of hypnotic reaction, like with snakes. After all, if you can charm a snake with music, then why not a cat? Except that millions of cats hear the stuff every day of their lives, on radio and gramophone and piano, and, as far as she knew, there'd never yet been a case of one behaving like this. This one was acting as though it were following every single note. It was certainly a fantastic thing.

But was it not also a wonderful thing? Indeed it was. In fact, unless she was much mistaken, it was a kind of miracle, one of those animal miracles that happen about once every hundred years.

'I could see you *loved* that one,' she said when the piece was over. 'Although I'm sorry I didn't play it any too well today. Which did you like best – the Vivaldi or the Schumann?'

The cat made no reply, so Louisa, fearing she might lose the attention of her listener, went straight into the next part of the programme – Liszt's second *Petrarch Sonnet*.

And now an extraordinary thing happened. She hadn't played more than three or four bars when the animal's whiskers began perceptibly to twitch. Slowly it drew itself up to an extra height, laid its head on one side, then on the other, and stared into space with a kind of frowning concentrated look that seemed to say, What's this? Don't tell me. I know it so well, but just for the moment I don't seem to be able to place it. Louisa was fascinated, and with her little mouth half open and half smiling, she continued to play, waiting to see what on earth was going to happen next.

The cat stood up, walked to one end of the sofa, sat down again, listened some more; then all at once it bounded to the floor and leaped up on to the piano bench beside her. There it sat, listening intently to the lovely sonnet, not dreamily this time, but very erect, the large yellow eyes fixed upon Louisa's fingers.

'Well!' she said as she struck the last chord. 'So you came up to sit beside me, did you? You like this better than the sofa? All right, I'll let you stay, but you must keep still and not jump about.' She put out a hand and stroked the cat softly along the back, from head to tail. 'That was Liszt,' she went on. 'Mind you, he can sometimes be quite horribly vulgar, but in things like this he's really charming.'

She was beginning to enjoy this odd animal pantomime, so she went straight on into the next item on the programme, Schumann's *Kinderszenen*.

She hadn't been playing for more than a minute or two when she realized that the cat had again moved, and was now back in its old place on the sofa. She'd been watching her hands at the time, and presumably that was why she hadn't even noticed its going; all the same, it must have been an extremely swift and silent move. The cat was still staring at her, still apparently attending closely to the music, and yet it seemed to Louisa that there was not now the same rapturous enthusiasm there'd been during the previous piece, the Liszt. In addition, the act of leaving the stool and returning to the sofa appeared in itself to be a mild but positive gesture of disappointment.

'What's the matter?' she asked when it was over. 'What's wrong with Schumann? What's so marvellous about Liszt?' The cat looked straight back at her with those yellow eyes that had small jet-black bars lying vertically in their centres.

This, she told herself, is really beginning to get interesting – a trifle spooky, too, when she came to think of it. But one look at the cat sitting there on the sofa, so bright and attentive, so obviously waiting for more music, quickly reassured her.

'All right,' she said. 'I'll tell you what I'm going to do. I'm going to alter my programme specially for you. You seem to like Liszt so much, I'll give you another.'

She hesitated, searching her memory for a good Liszt; then softly she began to play one of the twelve little pieces from *Der Weihnachtsbaum*. She was now watching the cat very closely, and the first thing she noticed was that the whiskers again began to twitch. It jumped down to the carpet, stood still a moment, inclining its head, quivering with excitement, and then, with a slow, silky stride, it walked round the piano, hopped up on the bench, and sat down beside her.

They were in the middle of all this when Edward came in from the garden.

'Edward!' Louisa cried, jumping up. 'Oh, Edward, darling! Listen to this! Listen what's happened!'

'What is it now?' he said. 'I'd like some tea.' He had one of those narrow, sharp-nosed, faintly magenta faces, and the sweat was making it shine as though it were a long wet grape.

'It's the cat!' Louisa cried, pointing to it sitting quietly on the piano bench. 'Just *wait* till you hear what's happened!'

'I thought I told you to take it to the police.'

'But, Edward, *listen* to me. This is *terribly* exciting. This is a *musical* cat.'

'Oh yes?'

'This cat can appreciate music, and it can understand it too.'

'Now stop this nonsense, Louisa, and let's for God's sake have some tea. I'm hot and tired from cutting brambles and building bonfires.' He sat down in an armchair, took a cigarette from a box beside him and lit it with an immense patent lighter that stood near the box.

'What you don't understand,' Louisa said, 'is that something extremely exciting has been happening here in our own house while you were out, something that may even be . . . well . . . almost momentous.'

'I'm quite sure of that.'

'Edward, *please*!'

Louisa was standing by the piano, her little pink face pinker than ever, a scarlet rose high up on each cheek. 'If you want to know,' she said, 'I'll tell you what I think.'

'I'm listening, dear.'

'I think it might be possible that we are at this moment sitting in the presence of –' She stopped, as though suddenly sensing the absurdity of the thought.

'Yes?'

'You may think it silly, Edward, but it's honestly what I think.'

'In the presence of who, for heaven's sake?'

'Of Franz Liszt himself!'

Her husband took a long slow pull at his cigarette and blew the smoke up at the ceiling. He had the tight-skinned, concave cheeks of a man who has worn a full set of dentures for many years, and every time he sucked at a cigarette, the cheeks went in even more, and the bones of his face stood out like a skeleton's. 'I don't get you,' he said.

'Edward, listen to me. From what I've seen this afternoon with my own eyes, it really looks as though this might actually be some sort of a reincarnation.'

'You mean this lousy cat?'

'Don't talk like that, dear, please.'

'You're not ill, are you, Louisa?'

'I'm perfectly all right, thank you very much. I'm a bit confused – I don't mind admitting it, but who wouldn't be after what's just happened? Edward, I swear to you –'

'What *did* happen, if I may ask?'

Louisa told him, and all the while she was speaking, her husband lay sprawled in the chair with his legs stretched out in front of him, sucking at his cigarette and blowing the smoke up at the ceiling. There was a thin cynical smile on his mouth.

'I don't see anything very unusual about that,' he said when it was over. 'All it is – it's a trick cat. It's been taught tricks, that's all.'

'Don't be silly, Edward. Every time I play Liszt, he gets all excited and comes running over to sit on the stool beside me. But only for Liszt, and nobody can teach a cat the difference between Liszt and Schumann. You don't even know it yourself. But this one can do it every single time. Quite obscure Liszt, too.'

'Twice,' the husband said. 'He's only done it twice.'

'Twice is enough.'

'Let's see him do it again. Come on.'

'No,' Louisa said. 'Definitely not. Because if this *is* Liszt, as I believe it is, or anyway the soul of Liszt or whatever it is that comes back, then it's certainly not right or even very kind to put him through a lot of silly undignified tests.'

'My dear woman! This is a *cat* – a rather stupid grey cat

that nearly got its coat singed by the bonfire, this morning in the garden. And, anyway, what do you know about reincarnation?'

'If his soul is there, that's enough for me,' Louisa said firmly. 'That's all that counts.'

'Come on, then. Let's see him perform. Let's see him tell the difference between his own stuff and someone else's.'

'No, Edward. I've told you before. I refuse to put him through any more silly circus tests. He's had quite enough of that for one day. But I'll tell you what I *will* do. I'll play him a little more of his own music.'

'A fat lot that'll prove.'

'You watch. And one thing is certain – as soon as he recognizes it, he'll refuse to budge off that bench where he's sitting now.'

Louisa went to the music shelf, took down a book of Liszt, thumbed through it quickly, and chose another of his finger compositions – the B minor sonata. She had meant to play only the first part of the work, but once she got started and saw how the cat was sitting there literally quivering with pleasure and watching her hands with that rapturous concentrated look, she didn't have the heart to stop. She played it all the way through. When it was finished, she glanced up at her husband and smiled. 'There you are,' she said. 'You can't tell me he wasn't absolutely *loving* it.'

'He just likes the noise, that's all.'

'He was *loving* it. Weren't you, darling?' she said, lifting the cat in her arms. 'Oh my goodness, if only he could talk. Just think of it, dear – he met Beethoven in his youth! He knew Schubert and Mendelssohn and Schumann and Berlioz and Grieg and Delacroix and Ingres and Heine and Balzac. And let me see . . . My heavens, he was Wagner's father-in-law! I'm holding Wagner's father-in-law in my arms!'

'Louisa!' her husband said sharply, sitting up straight. 'Pull yourself together.' There was a new edge to his voice now, and he spoke louder.

Louisa glanced up quickly. 'Edward, I do believe you're jealous!'

'Oh sure, sure I'm jealous – of a lousy grey cat!'

'Then don't be so grumpy and cynical about it all. If you're going to behave like this, the best thing you can do is to go back to your gardening and leave the two of us together in peace. That will be best for all of us, won't it, darling?' she said, addressing the cat, stroking its head. 'And later on this evening, we shall have some more music together, you and I, some more of your own work. Oh yes,' she said, kissing the creature several times on the neck, 'and we might have a little Chopin, too. You needn't tell me – I happen to know you adore Chopin. You used to be great friends with him, didn't you, darling? As a matter of fact – if I remember rightly – it was in Chopin's apartment that you met the great love of your life, Madame Something-or-other. Had three illegitimate children by her, too, didn't you? Yes, you did, you naughty thing, and don't go trying to deny it. So you shall have some Chopin,' she said, kissing the cat again, 'and that'll probably bring back all sorts of lovely memories to you, won't it?'

'Louisa, stop this at once!'

'Oh, don't be so stuffy, Edward.'

'You're behaving like a perfect idiot, woman. And anyway, you forget we're going out this evening, to Bill and Betty's for canasta.'

'Oh, but I couldn't *possibly* go out now. There's no question of that.'

Edward got up slowly from his chair, then bent down and stubbed his cigarette hard into the ashtray. 'Tell me something,' he said quietly. 'You don't really believe this – this twaddle you're talking, do you?'

'But of *course* I do. I don't think there's any question about it now. And, what's more, I consider that it puts a tremendous responsibility upon us, Edward – upon both of us. You as well.'

'You know what I think,' he said. 'I think you ought to see a doctor. And damn quick too.'

With that, he turned and stalked out of the room, through the French windows, back into the garden.

Louisa watched him striding across the lawn towards his bonfire and his brambles, and she waited until he was out of sight before she turned and ran to the front door, still carrying the cat.

Soon she was in the car, driving to town.

She parked in front of the library, locked the cat in the car, hurried up the steps into the building and headed straight for the reference room. There she began searching the cards for books on two subjects – REINCARNATION and LISZT.

Under REINCARNATION she found something called *Recurring Earth-Lives – How and Why*, by a man called F. Milton Willis, published in 1921. Under LISZT she found two biographical volumes. She took out all three books, returned to the car and drove home.

Back in the house, she placed the cat on the sofa, sat herself down beside it with her three books and prepared to do some serious reading. She would begin, she decided, with Mr F. Milton Willis's work. The volume was thin and a trifle soiled, but it had a good heavy feel to it, and the author's name had an authoritative ring.

The doctrine of reincarnation, she read, states that spiritual souls pass from higher to higher forms of animals. 'A man can, for instance, no more be reborn as an animal than an adult can re-become a child.'

She read this again. But how did he know? How could he be so sure? He couldn't. No one could possibly be certain about a thing like that. At the same time, the statement took a great deal of the wind out of her sails.

'Around the centre of consciousness of each of us, there are, besides the dense outer body, four other bodies, invisible to the eye of flesh, but perfectly visible to people whose faculties of perception of superphysical things have undergone the requisite development . . .'

She didn't understand that one at all, but she read on, and soon she came to an interesting passage that told how long a soul usually stayed away from the earth before

returning in someone else's body. The time varied according to type, and Mr Willis gave the following breakdown:

Drunkards and the unemployable	40/50	YEARS
Unskilled labourers	60/100	"
Skilled workers	100/200	"
The bourgeoisie	200/300	"
The upper-middle classes	500	"
The highest class of gentleman farmers	600/1,000	"
Those in the Path of Initiation	1,500/2,000	"

Quickly she referred to one of the other books, to find
out how long Liszt had been dead. It said he died in Bay-
reuth in 1886. That was sixty-seven years ago. Therefore,
according to Mr Willis, he'd have to have been an unskilled
labourer to come back so soon. That didn't seem to fit at
all. On the other hand, she didn't think much of the
author's methods of grading. According to him, 'the high-
est class of gentleman farmer' was just about the most
superior being on the earth. Red jackets and stirrup cups
and the bloody, sadistic murder of the fox. No, she
thought, that isn't right. It was a pleasure to find herself
beginning to doubt Mr Willis.

Later in the book, she came upon a list of some of the
more famous reincarnations. Epictetus, she was told,
returned to earth as Ralph Waldo Emerson. Cicero came
back as Gladstone, Alfred the Great as Queen Victoria,
William the Conqueror as Lord Kitchener. Ashoka Vardhana, King of India in 272 BC, came back as Colonel

Henry Steel Olcott, an esteemed American lawyer. Pythagoras returned as Master Koot Hoomi, the gentleman who founded the Theosophical Society with Mme Blavatsky and Colonel H. S. Olcott (the esteemed American lawyer, alias Ashoka Vardhana, King of India). It didn't say who Mme Blavatsky had been. But 'Theodore Roosevelt,' it said.

> has for numbers of incarnations played great parts as a leader of men . . . From him descended the royal line of ancient Chaldea, he having been, about 30,000 BC, appointed Governor of Chaldea by the Ego we know as Caesar who was then ruler of Persia . . . Roosevelt and Caesar have been together time after time as military and administrative leaders; at one time, many thousands of years ago, they were husband and wife . . .

That was enough for Louisa. Mr F. Milton Willis was clearly nothing but a guesser. She was not impressed by his dogmatic assertions. The fellow was probably on the right track, but his pronouncements were extravagant, especially the first one of all, about animals. Soon she hoped to be able to confound the whole Theosophical Society with her proof that man could indeed reappear as a lower animal. Also that he did not have to be an unskilled labourer to come back within a hundred years.

She now turned to one of the Liszt biographies, and she was glancing through it casually when her husband came in again from the garden.

'What are you doing now?' he asked.

'Oh – just checking up a little here and there. Listen, my dear, did you know that Theodore Roosevelt once was Caesar's wife?'

'Louisa,' he said, 'look – why don't we stop this nonsense? I don't like to see you making a fool of yourself like this. Just give me that goddam cat and I'll take it to the police station myself.'

Louisa didn't seem to hear him. She was staring openmouthed at a picture of Liszt in the book that lay on her lap. 'My God!' she cried. 'Edward, look!'

'What?'

'Look! The warts on his face! I forgot all about them! He had these great warts on his face and it was a famous thing. Even his students used to cultivate little tufts of hair on their own faces in the same spots, just to be like him.'

'What's that got to do with it?'

'Nothing. I mean, not the students. But the warts have.'

'Oh Christ,' the man said. 'Oh Christ God Almighty.'

'The cat has them, too! Look, I'll show you.'

She took the animal on to her lap and began examining its face. 'There! There's one! And there's another! Wait a minute! I do believe they're in the same places! Where's that picture?'

It was a famous portrait of the musician in his old age, showing the fine powerful face framed in a mass of long grey hair that covered his ears and came halfway down his neck. On the face itself, each large wart had been faithfully reproduced, and there were five of them in all.

'Now, in the picture there's *one* above the right eyebrow.'

She looked above the right eyebrow of the cat. 'Yes! It's there! In exactly the same place! And another on the left, at the top of the nose. That one's there, too! And one just below it on the cheek. And two fairly close together under the chin on the right side. Edward! Edward! Come and look! They're exactly the same.'

'It doesn't prove a thing.'

She looked up at her husband, who was standing in the centre of the room in his green sweater and khaki slacks, still perspiring freely. 'You're scared, aren't you, Edward? Scared of losing your precious dignity and having people think you might be making a fool of yourself just for once.'

'I refuse to get hysterical about it, that's all.'

Louisa turned back to the book and began reading some more. 'This is interesting,' she said. 'It says here that Liszt loved all of Chopin's works except one – the scherzo in B flat minor. Apparently he hated that. He called it the "Governess Scherzo", and said that it ought to be reserved solely for people in that profession.'

'So what?'

'Edward, listen. As you insist on being so horrid about all this, I'll tell you what I'm going to do. I'm going to play this scherzo right now and you can stay here and see what happens.'

'And then maybe you will deign to get us some supper.'

Louisa got up and took from the shelf a large green volume containing all of Chopin's works. 'Here it is. Oh yes, I remember it. It *is* rather awful. Now, listen – or, rather, watch. Watch to see what he does.'

She placed the music on the piano and sat down. Her husband remained standing. He had his hands in his pockets and a cigarette in his mouth, and in spite of himself he was watching the cat, which was now dozing on the sofa. When Louisa began to play, the first effect was as dramatic as ever. The animal jumped up as though it had been stung, and it stood motionless for at least a minute, the ears pricked up, the whole body quivering. Then it became restless and began to walk back and forth along the length of the sofa. Finally, it hopped down on to the floor, and with its nose and tail held high in the air, it marched slowly, majestically, from the room.

'There!' Louisa cried, jumping up and running after it. 'That does it! That really proves it!' She came back, carrying the cat, which she put down again on the sofa. Her whole face was shining with excitement now, her fists were clenched white, and the little bun on top of her head was loosening and going over to one side. 'What about it, Edward? What d'you think?' She was laughing nervously as she spoke.

'I must say it was quite amusing.'

'*Amusing!* My dear Edward, it's the most wonderful thing that's ever happened! Oh, goodness me!' she cried, picking up the cat again and hugging it to her bosom. 'Isn't it marvellous to think we've got Franz Liszt staying in the house?'

'Now, Louisa. Don't let's get hysterical.'

'I can't help it, I simply can't. And to *imagine* that he's actually going to live with us for always!'

'I beg your pardon?'

'Oh, Edward! I can hardly talk from excitement. And d'you know what I'm going to do next? Every musician in the whole world is going to want to meet him, that's a fact, and ask him about the people he knew – about Beethoven and Chopin and Schubert –'

'He can't talk,' her husband said.

'Well – all right. But they're going to want to meet him anyway, just to see him and touch him and to play their music to him, modern music he's never heard before.'

'He wasn't that great. Now, if it had been Bach or Beethoven . . .'

'Don't interrupt, Edward, please. So what I'm going to do is to notify all the important living composers everywhere. It's my duty. I'll tell them Liszt is here, and invite them to visit him. And you know what? They'll come flying in from every corner of the earth!'

'To see a grey cat?'

'Darling, it's the same thing. It's *him*. No one cares what he *looks* like. Oh, Edward, it'll be the most exciting thing there ever was!'

'They'll think you're mad.'

'You wait and see.' She was holding the cat in her arms and petting it tenderly but looking across at her husband, who now walked over to the French windows and stood there staring out into the garden. The evening was beginning, and the lawn was turning slowly from green to black, and in the distance he could see the smoke from his bonfire rising straight up in a white column.

'No,' he said, without turning round, 'I'm not having it. Not in this house. It'll make us both look perfect fools.'

'Edward, what do you mean?'

'Just what I say. I absolutely refuse to have you stirring up a lot of publicity about a foolish thing like this. You happen to have found a trick cat. OK – that's fine. Keep it, if it pleases you. I don't mind. But I don't wish you to go any farther than that. Do you understand me, Louisa?'

'Farther than what?'

'I don't want to hear any more of this crazy talk. You're acting like a lunatic.'

Louisa put the cat slowly down on the sofa. Then slowly she raised herself to her full small height and took one pace forward. '*Damn* you, Edward!' she shouted, stamping her foot. 'For the first time in our lives something really exciting comes along and you're scared to death of having anything to do with it because someone may laugh at you! That's right, isn't it? You can't deny it, can you?'

'Louisa,' her husband said. 'That's quite enough of that. Pull yourself together now and stop this at once.' He walked over and took a cigarette from the box on the table, then lit it with the enormous patent lighter. His wife stood watching him, and now the tears were beginning to trickle out of the inside corners of her eyes, making two little shiny rivers where they ran through the powder on her cheeks.

'We've been having too many of these scenes just lately, Louisa,' he was saying. 'No no, don't interrupt. Listen to me. I make full allowance for the fact that this may be an awkward time of life for you, and that –'

24

'Oh my God! You idiot! You pompous idiot! Can't you see that this is different, this is – this is something miraculous? Can't you see *that*?'

At that point, he came across the room and took her firmly by the shoulders. He had the freshly lit cigarette between his lips, and she could see faint contours on his skin where the heavy perspiration had dried in patches. 'Listen,' he said. 'I'm hungry. I've given up my golf and I've been working all day in the garden, and I'm tired and hungry and I want some supper. So do you. Off you go now to the kitchen and get us both something good to eat.'

Louisa stepped back and put both hands to her mouth. 'My heavens!' she cried. 'I forgot all about it. He must be absolutely famished. Except for some milk, I haven't given him a thing to eat since he arrived.'

'Who?'

'Why, *him*, of course. I must go at once and cook something really special. I wish I knew what his favourite dishes used to be. What do you think he would like best, Edward?'

'*Goddam* it, Louisa!'

'Now, Edward, please. I'm going to handle this *my* way just for once. You stay here,' she said, bending down and touching the cat gently with her fingers. 'I won't be long.'

Louisa went into the kitchen and stood for a moment, wondering what special dish she might prepare. How about a soufflé? A nice cheese soufflé? Yes, that would be rather special. Of course, Edward didn't much care for them, but that couldn't be helped.

She was only a fair cook, and she couldn't be sure of always having a soufflé come out well, but she took extra trouble this time and waited a long while to make certain the oven had heated fully to the correct temperature. While the soufflé was baking and she was searching around for something to go with it, it occurred to her that Liszt had probably never in his life tasted either avocado pears or grapefruit, so she decided to give him both of them at once in a salad. It would be fun to watch his reaction. It really would.

When it was all ready, she put it on a tray and carried it into the living-room. At the exact moment she entered, she saw her husband coming in through the French windows from the garden.

'Here's his supper,' she said, putting it on the table and turning towards the sofa. 'Where is he?'

Her husband closed the garden door behind him and walked across the room to get himself a cigarette.

'Edward, where is he?'

'Who?'

'You know who.'

'Ah, yes. Yes, that's right. Well – I'll tell you.' He was bending forward to light the cigarette, and his hands were cupped around the enormous patent lighter. He glanced up and saw Louisa looking at him – at his shoes and the bottoms of his khaki slacks, which were damp from walking in the long grass.

'I just went to see how the bonfire was going,' he said.

Her eyes travelled slowly upwards and rested on his hands.

'It's still burning fine,' he went on. 'I think it'll keep going all night.'

But the way she was staring made him uncomfortable.

'What is it?' he said, lowering the lighter. Then he looked down and noticed for the first time the long thin scratch that ran diagonally clear across the back of one hand, from the knuckle to the wrist.

'*Edward!*'

'Yes,' he said, 'I know. Those brambles are terrible. They tear you to pieces. Now, just a minute, Louisa. What's the matter?'

'*Edward!*'

'Oh, for God's sake, woman, sit down and keep calm. There's nothing to get worked up about. Louisa! Louisa, *sit down*!'

Katina

First published in *Ladies' Home Journal*
(March 1944)

*Some brief notes about the last days of
RAF fighters in the first Greek campaign.*

Peter saw her first.

She was sitting on a stone, quite still, with her hands resting on her lap. She was staring vacantly ahead, seeing nothing, and all around, up and down the little street, people were running backwards and forwards with buckets of water, emptying them through the windows of the burning houses.

Across the street on the cobblestones, there was a dead boy. Someone had moved his body close in to the side so that it would not be in the way.

A little farther down an old man was working on a pile of stones and rubble. One by one he was carrying the stones away and dumping them to the side. Sometimes he would bend down and peer into the ruins, repeating a name over and over again.

All around there was shouting and running and fires and buckets of water and dust. And the girl sat quietly on the stone, staring ahead, not moving. There was blood running down the left side of her face. It ran down from her forehead and dripped from her chin on to the dirty print dress she was wearing.

Peter saw her and said, 'Look at that little girl.'

We went up to her and Fin put his hand on her shoulder, bending down to examine the cut. 'Looks like a piece of shrapnel,' he said. 'She ought to see the Doc.'

Peter and I made a chair with our hands and Fin lifted her up on to it. We started back through the streets and out towards the aerodrome, the two of us walking a little awkwardly, bending down, facing our burden. I could feel Peter's fingers clasped tightly in mine and I could feel the buttocks of the little girl resting lightly on my wrists. I was on the left side and the blood was dripping down from her face on to the arm of my flying suit, running down the waterproof cloth on to the back of my hand. The girl never moved or said anything.

Fin said, 'She's bleeding rather fast. We'd better walk a bit quicker.'

I couldn't see much of her face because of the blood, but I could tell that she was lovely. She had high cheekbones and large round eyes, pale blue like an autumn sky, and her hair was short and fair. I guessed she was about nine years old.

This was in Greece in early April 1941, at Paramythia. Our fighter squadron was stationed on a muddy field near the village. We were in a deep valley and all around us were the mountains. The freezing winter had passed, and now, almost before anyone knew it, spring had come. It had come quietly and swiftly, melting the ice on the lakes and brushing the snow off the mountain tops; and all over the airfield we could see the pale-green shoots of grass pushing up through the mud, making a carpet for our landings. In our valley there were warm winds and wild flowers.

The Germans, who had pushed in through Yugoslavia a few days before, were now operating in force, and that afternoon they had come over very high with about thirty-five Dorniers and bombed the village. Peter and Fin and I were off duty for a while, and the three of us had gone down to see if there was anything we could do in the way of rescue work. We had spent a few hours digging around in the ruins and helping to put out fires, and we were on our way back when we saw the girl.

Now, as we approached the landing field, we could see the Hurricanes circling around coming in to land, and there was the Doc standing out in front of the dispersal tent, just as he should have been, waiting to see if anyone had been hurt. We walked towards him, carrying the child, and Fin, who was a few yards in front, said, 'Doc, you lazy old devil, here's a job for you.'

The Doc was young and kind and morose except when he got drunk. When he got drunk he sang very well.

'Take her into the sick bay,' he said. Peter and I carried her in and put her down on a chair. Then we left her and wandered over to the dispersal tent to see how the boys had got along.

It was beginning to get dark. There was a sunset behind the ridge over in the west, and there was a full moon, a bombers' moon, climbing up into the sky. The moon shone upon the shoulders of the tents and made them white; small white pyramids, standing up straight, clustering in little orderly groups around the edges of the aerodrome. They had a scared-sheep look about them the way they clustered themselves together, and they had a human look about them the way they stood up close to one another, and it seemed almost as though they knew that there was going to be trouble, as though someone had warned them that they might be forgotten and left behind. Even as I looked, I thought I saw them move. I thought I saw them huddle just a fraction nearer together.

And then, silently, without a sound, the mountains crept a little closer into our valley.

For the next two days there was much flying. There was the getting up at dawn, there was the flying, the fighting and the sleeping; and there was the retreat of the Army. That was about all there was or all there was time for. But on the third day the clouds dropped down over the mountains and slid into the valley. And it rained, so we sat around in the mess-tent drinking beer and resinato, while the rain made a noise like a sewing machine on the roof. Then lunch. For the first time in days the whole squadron was present. Fifteen pilots at a long table with benches on either side and Monkey, the CO, sitting at the head.

We were still in the middle of our fried corned beef when the flap of the tent opened and in came the Doc with an enormous dripping raincoat over his head. And with him, under the coat, was the little girl. She had a bandage round her head.

The Doc said, 'Hello. I've brought a guest.' We looked around and suddenly, automatically, we all stood up.

The Doc was taking off his raincoat and the little girl

was standing there with her hands hanging loose by her sides looking at the men, and the men were all looking at her. With her fair hair and pale skin she looked less like a Greek than anyone I've ever seen. She was frightened by the fifteen scruffy-looking foreigners who had suddenly stood up when she came in, and for a moment she half turned as if she were going to run away out into the rain.

Monkey said, 'Hallo. Hallo there. Come and sit down.'

'Talk Greek,' the Doc said. 'She doesn't understand.'

Fin and Peter and I looked at one another and Fin said, 'Good God, it's our little girl. Nice work, Doc.'

She recognized Fin and walked round to where he was standing. He took her by the hand and sat her down on the bench, and everyone else sat down too. We gave her some fried corned beef and she ate it slowly, looking down at her plate while she ate. Monkey said, 'Get Pericles.'

Pericles was the Greek interpreter attached to the squadron. He was a wonderful man we'd picked up at Yanina, where he had been the local schoolteacher. He had been out of work ever since the war started. 'The children do not come to school,' he said. 'They are up in the mountains and fight. I cannot teach sums to the stones.'

Pericles came in. He was old, with a beard, a long pointed nose and sad grey eyes. You couldn't see his mouth, but his beard had a way of smiling when he talked.

'Ask her her name,' said Monkey.

He said something to her in Greek. She looked up and said, 'Katina.' That was all she said.

'Look, Pericles,' Peter said, 'ask her what she was doing sitting by that heap of ruins in the village.'

Fin said, 'For God's sake, leave her alone.'

'Ask her, Pericles,' said Peter.

'What should I ask?' said Pericles, frowning.

Peter said, 'What she was doing sitting on that heap of stuff in the village when we found her.'

Pericles sat down on the bench beside her and he talked to her again. He spoke gently and you could see that his beard was smiling a little as he spoke, helping her. She listened and it seemed a long time before she answered. When she spoke, it was only a few words, and the old man translated: 'She says that her family were under the stones.'

Outside the rain was coming down harder than ever. It beat upon the roof of the mess-tent so that the canvas shivered as the water bounced upon it. I got up and walked over and lifted the flap of the tent. The mountains were invisible behind the rain, but I knew they were around us on every side. I had a feeling that they were laughing at us, laughing at the smallness of our numbers and at the hopeless courage of the pilots. I felt that it was the mountains, not us, who were the clever ones. Had not the hills that very morning turned and looked north-wards towards Tepelene, where they had seen a thousand German aircraft gathered under the shadow of Olympus? Was it not true that the snow on the top of Dodona had melted away in a day, sending little rivers of water running down across our landing field? Had not Kataphidi buried his head in a cloud so that our pilots might be tempted to fly through the whiteness and crash against his rugged shoulders?

And as I stood there looking at the rain through the tent flap, I knew for certain that the mountains had turned against us. I could feel it in my stomach.

I went back into the tent and there was Fin, sitting beside Katina, trying to teach her English words. I don't know whether he made much progress, but I do know that once he made her laugh and that was a wonderful thing for him to have done. I remember the sudden sound of her high laughter and how we all looked up and saw her face; how we saw how different it was to what it had been before. No one but Fin could have done it. He was so gay himself that it was difficult to be serious in his presence. He was gay and tall and black-haired, and he was sitting there on the bench, leaning forward, whispering and smiling, teaching Katina to speak English and teaching her how to laugh.

The next day the skies cleared and once again we saw the mountains. We did a patrol over the troops which were already retreating slowly towards Thermopylae, and we met some Messerschmitts and Ju-87s dive-bombing the soldiers. I think we got a few of them, but they got Sandy. I saw him going down. I sat quite still for thirty seconds and watched his plane spiralling gently downwards. I sat and waited for the parachute. I remember switching over my radio and saying quietly, 'Sandy, you must jump now. You must jump; you're getting near the ground.' But there was no parachute.

When we landed and taxied in, there was Katina, standing outside the dispersal tent with the Doc; a tiny shrimp of a girl in a dirty print dress, standing there watching the machines as they came in to land. To Fin, as he walked in, she said, '*Tha girisis xana.*'

Fin said, 'What does it mean, Pericles?'

'It just means "You are back again,"' and he smiled.

The child had counted the aircraft on her fingers as they took off, and now she noticed that there was one missing. We were standing around taking off our parachutes and she was trying to ask us about it, when suddenly someone said, 'Look out. Here they come.' They came through a gap in the hills, a mass of thin, black silhouettes, coming down upon the aerodrome.

There was a scramble for the slit trenches and I remember seeing Fin catch Katina round the waist and carry her off with us, and I remember seeing her fight like a tiger the whole way to the trenches.

As soon as we got into the trench and Fin had let her go, she jumped out and ran over on to the airfield. Down came the Messerschmitts with their guns blazing, swooping so low that you could see the noses of the pilots sticking out under their goggles. Their bullets threw up spurts of dust all around and I saw one of our Hurricanes burst into flames. I saw Katina standing right in the middle of the field, standing firmly with her legs astride and her back to us, looking up at the Germans as they dived past. I have never seen anything smaller and more angry and more fierce in my life. She seemed to be shouting at them, but the noise was great and one could hear

35

nothing at all except the engines and the guns of the aeroplanes.

Then it was over. It was over as quickly as it had begun, and no one said very much except Fin, who said, 'I wouldn't have done that, ever; not even if I was crazy.'

That evening Monkey got out the squadron records and added Katina's name to the list of members, and the equipment officer was ordered to provide a tent for her. So, on 11 April 1941, she became a member of the squadron.

In two days she knew the first name or nickname of every pilot and Fin had already taught her to say 'Any luck?' and 'Nice work.'

But that was a time of much activity, and when I try to think of it hour by hour, the whole period becomes hazy in my mind. Mostly, I remember, it was escorting the Blenheims to Valona, and if it wasn't that, it was a ground-strafe of Italian trucks on the Albanian border or an SOS from the Northumberland Regiment saying they were having the hell bombed out of them by half the aircraft in Europe.

None of that can I remember. I can remember nothing of that time clearly, save for two things. The one was Katina and how she was with us all the time; how she was everywhere and how wherever she went the people were pleased to see her. The other thing that I remember was when the Bull came into the mess-tent one evening after a lone patrol. The Bull was an enormous man with massive, slightly hunched shoulders and his chest was like the top of an oak table. Before the war he had done many things, most of them things which one could not do unless one conceded beforehand that there was no difference between life and death. He was quiet and casual and when he came into a room or into a tent, he always looked as though he had made a mistake and hadn't really meant to come in at all. It was getting dark and we were sitting round in the tent playing shove-halfpenny when the Bull came in. We knew that he had just landed.

He glanced around a little apologetically, then he said, 'Hello,' and wandered over to the bar and began to get out a bottle of beer.

Someone said, 'See anything, Bull?'

The Bull said, 'Yes,' and went on fiddling with the bottle of beer.

I suppose we were all very interested in our game of shove-halfpenny because no one said anything else for about five minutes. Then Peter said, 'What did you see, Bull?'

The Bull was leaning against the bar, alternately sipping his beer and trying to make a hooting noise by blowing down the neck of the empty bottle.

Peter said, 'What did you see?'

The Bull put down the bottle and looked up. 'Five S-79s,' he said.

I remember hearing him say it, but I remember also that our game was exciting and that Fin had one more shove to win. We all watched him miss it and Peter said, 'Fin, I think you're going to lose.' And Fin said, 'Go to hell.'

We finished the game, then I looked up and saw the

Bull still leaning against the bar making noises with his beer bottle.

He said, 'This sounds like the old *Mauretania* coming into New York harbour,' and he started blowing into the bottle again.

'What happened with the S-79s?' I said.

He stopped his blowing and put down the bottle.

'I shot them down.'

Everyone heard it. At that moment eleven pilots in that tent stopped what they were doing and eleven heads flicked around and looked at the Bull. He took another drink of his beer and said quietly, 'At one time I counted eighteen parachutes in the air together.'

A few days later he went on patrol and did not come back.

Shortly afterwards Monkey got a message from Athens. It said that the squadron was to move down to Elevsis and from there do a defence of Athens itself and also cover the troops retreating through the Thermopylae Pass.

Katina was to go with the trucks and we told the Doc he was to see that she arrived safely. It would take them a day to make the journey. We flew over the mountains towards the south, fourteen of us, and at two thirty we landed at Elevsis. It was a lovely aerodrome with runways and hangars; and best of all, Athens was only twenty-five minutes away by car.

That evening, as it was getting dark, I stood outside my tent. I stood with my hands in my pockets watching the sun go down and thinking of the work which we were to do. The more that I thought of it, the more impossible I knew it to be. I looked up, and once again I saw the mountains. They were closer to us here, crowding in upon us on all sides, standing shoulder to shoulder, tall and naked, with their heads in the clouds, surrounding us everywhere save in the south, where lay Piraeus and the open sea. I knew that each night, when it was very dark, when we were all tired and sleeping in our tents, those mountains would move forward, creeping a little closer, making no noise, until at last on the appointed day they would tumble forward with one great rush and push us into the sea.

Fin emerged from his tent.

'Have you seen the mountains?' I said.

'They're full of gods. They aren't any good,' he answered.

'I wish they'd stand still,' I said.

Fin looked up at the great crags of Parnes and Pentelikon.

'They're full of gods,' he said. 'Sometimes, in the middle of the night, when there is a moon, you can see the gods sitting on the summits. There was one on Kataphidi when we were at Paramythia. He was huge, like a house but without any shape and quite black.'

'You saw him?'

'Of course I saw him.'

'When?' I said. 'When did you see him, Fin?'

Fin said, 'Let's go into Athens. Let's go and look at the women in Athens.'

The next day the trucks carrying the ground staff and the equipment rumbled on to the aerodrome, and there was Katina sitting in the front seat of the leading vehicle with the Doc beside her. She waved to us as she jumped down, and she came running towards us, laughing and calling our names in a curious Greek way. She still had on the same dirty print dress and she still had a bandage round her forehead; but the sun was shining in her hair.

We showed her the tent which we had prepared for her and we showed her the small cotton nightdress which Fin had obtained in some mysterious way the night before in Athens. It was white with a lot of little blue birds embroidered on the front and we all thought that it was very beautiful. Katina wanted to put it on at once and it took a long time to persuade her that it was meant only for sleeping in. Six times Fin had to perform a complicated act which consisted of pretending to put on the nightdress, then jumping on to the bed and falling fast asleep. In the end she nodded vigorously and understood.

For the next two days nothing happened, except that the remnants of another squadron came down from the north and joined us. They brought six Hurricanes, so that altogether we had about twenty machines.

Then we waited.

On the third day German reconnaissance aircraft appeared, circling high over Piraeus, and we chased after them but never got up in time to catch them. This was understandable, because our radar was of a very special type. It is obsolete now, and I doubt whether it will ever be used again. All over the country, in all the villages, up on the mountains and out on the islands, there were

Greeks, all of whom were connected to our small operations room by field telephone.

We had no operations officer, so we took it in turns to be on duty for the day. My turn came on the fourth day, and I remember clearly what happened.

At six thirty in the morning the phone buzzed.

'This is A-7,' said a very Greek voice. 'This is A-7. There are noises overhead.'

I looked at the map. There was a little ring with 'A-7' written inside it just beside Yanina. I put a cross on the celluloid which covered the map and wrote 'Noises' beside it, as well as the time: '0631 hours.'

Three minutes later the phone went again.

'This is A-4. This is A-4. There are many noises above me,' said an old quavering voice, 'but I cannot see because there are thick clouds.'

I looked at the map. A-4 was Mount Karava. I made another cross on the celluloid and wrote 'Many noises – 0634,' and then I drew a line between Yanina and Karava. It pointed towards Athens, so I signalled the 'readiness' crew to scramble, and they took off and circled the city. Later they saw a Ju-88 on reconnaissance high above them, but they never caught it. It was in such a way that one worked the radar.

That evening when I came off duty I could not help thinking of the old Greek, sitting all alone in a hut up at A-4; sitting on the slope of Karava looking up into the whiteness and listening all day and all night for noises in the sky. I imagined the eagerness with which he seized the telephone when he heard something, and the joy he must have felt when the voice at the other end repeated his message and thanked him. I thought of his clothes and wondered if they were warm enough and I thought, for some reason, of his boots, which almost certainly had no soles left upon them and were stuffed with tree bark and paper.

That was April seventeenth. It was the evening when Monkey said, 'They say the Germans are at Lamia, which means that we're within range of their fighters. Tomorrow the fun should start.'

It did. At dawn the bombers came over, with the fighters circling around overhead, watching the bombers, waiting to pounce, but doing nothing unless someone interfered with the bombers.

I think we got eight Hurricanes into the air just before they arrived. It was not my turn to go up, so with Katina standing by my side I watched the battle from the ground. The child never said a word. Now and again she moved her head as she followed the little specks of silver dancing high above in the sky. I saw a plane coming down in a trail of black smoke and I looked at Katina. The hatred which was on the face of the child was the fierce burning hatred of an old woman who has hatred in her heart; it was an old woman's hatred and it was strange to see it.

In that battle we lost a sergeant called Donald.

At noon Monkey got another message from Athens. It said that morale was bad in the capital and that every available Hurricane was to fly in formation low over the city in order to show the inhabitants how strong we were and how many aircraft we had. Eighteen of us took off. We flew in tight formation up and down the main streets just above the roofs of the houses. I could see the people looking up, shielding their eyes from the sun, looking at us as we flew over, and in one street I saw an old woman who never looked up at all. None of them waved, and I knew then that they were resigned to their fate. None of them waved, and I knew, although I could not see their faces, that they were not even glad as we flew past.

Then we headed out towards Thermopylae, but on the way we circled the Acropolis twice. It was the first time I had seen it so close.

I saw a little hill – a mound almost, it seemed – and on the top of it I saw the white columns. There were a great number of them, grouped together in perfect order, not crowding one another, white in the sunshine, and I wondered, as I looked at them, how anyone could have put so much on top of so small a hill in such an elegant way.

Then we flew up the great Thermopylae Pass and I saw long lines of vehicles moving slowly southwards towards the sea. I saw occasional puffs of white smoke where a shell landed in the valley and I saw a direct hit on the road which made a gap in the line of trucks. But we saw no enemy aircraft.

When we landed Monkey said, 'Refuel quickly and get in the air again; I think they're waiting to catch us on the ground.'

But it was no use. They came down out of the sky five minutes after we had landed. I remember I was in the pilots' room in Number Two Hangar, talking to Fin and to a big tall man with rumpled hair called Paddy. We heard the bullets on the corrugated-iron roof of the hangar, then we heard explosions and the three of us dived under the little wooden table in the middle of the room. But the table upset. Paddy set it up again and crawled underneath. 'There's something about being under a table,' he said. 'I don't feel safe unless I'm under a table.'

Fin said, 'I never feel safe.' He was sitting on the floor watching the bullets making holes in the corrugated-iron wall of the room. There was a great clatter as the bullets hit the tin.

Then we became brave and got up and peeped outside the door. There were many Messerschmitt 109s circling the aerodrome, and one by one they straightened out and dived past the hangars, spraying the ground with their guns. But they did something else. They slid back their cockpit hoods and as they came past they threw out small bombs which exploded when they hit the ground and fiercely flung quantities of large lead balls in every direction. Those were the explosions which we had heard, and it was a great noise that the lead balls made as they hit the hangar.

Then I saw the men, the ground crews, standing up in their slit trenches firing at the Messerschmitts with rifles, reloading and firing as fast as they could, cursing and shouting as they shot, aiming ludicrously, hopelessly, aiming at an aeroplane with just a rifle. At Elevsis there were no other defences.

Suddenly the Messerschmitts all turned and headed for home, all except one, which glided down and made a smooth belly landing on the aerodrome.

Then there was chaos. The Greeks around us raised a shout and jumped on to the fire tender and headed out towards the crashed German aeroplane. At the same time more Greeks streamed out from every corner of the field, shouting and yelling and crying for the blood of the pilot. It was a mob intent upon vengeance and one could not blame them; but there were other considerations. We wanted the pilot for questioning, and we wanted him alive.

Monkey, who was standing on the tarmac, shouted to us, and Fin and Paddy and I raced with him towards the station wagon which was standing fifty yards away. Monkey was inside like a flash, started the engine and drove off just as the three of us jumped on the running board. The fire tender with the Greeks on it was not fast and it still had two hundred yards to go, and the other people had a long way to run. Monkey drove quickly and we beat them by about fifty yards.

We jumped up and ran over to the Messerschmitt, and there, sitting in the cockpit, was a fair-haired boy with pink cheeks and blue eyes. I have never seen anyone whose face showed so much fear.

He said to Monkey in English, 'I am hit in the leg.'

We pulled him out of the cockpit and got him into the car, while the Greeks stood around watching. The bullet had shattered the bone in his shin.

We drove him back and as we handed him over to the Doc, I saw Katina standing close, looking at the face of the German. This kid of nine was standing there looking at the German and she could not speak; she could not even move. She clutched the skirt of her dress in her hands and stared at the man's face. 'There is a mistake somewhere,' she seemed to be saying. 'There must be a mistake. This one has pink cheeks and fair hair and blue eyes. This cannot possibly be one of them. This is an ordinary boy.' She watched him as they put him on a stretcher and carried him off, then she turned and ran across the grass to her tent.

In the evening at supper I ate my fried sardines, but I could not eat the bread or the cheese. For three days I had been conscious of my stomach, of a hollow feeling such as one gets just before an operation or while waiting to have a tooth out in the dentist's house. I had had it all day for three days, from the moment I woke up to the time I fell asleep. Peter was sitting opposite me and I asked him about it.

'I've had it for a week,' he said. 'It's good for the bowels. It loosens them.'

'German aircraft are like liver pills,' said Fin from the bottom of the table. 'They are very good for you, aren't they, Doc?'

The Doc said, 'Maybe you've had an overdose.'

'I have,' said Fin, 'I've had an overdose of German liver pills. I didn't read the instructions on the bottle. Take two before retiring.'

Peter said, 'I would love to retire.'

After supper three of us walked down to the hangars with Monkey, who said, 'I'm worried about this ground-strafing. They never attack the hangars because they know that we never put anything inside them. Tonight I think

46

we'll collect four of the aircraft and put them into Number Two Hangar.'

That was a good idea. Normally the Hurricanes were dispersed all over the edge of the aerodrome, but they were being picked off one by one, because it was impossible to be in the air the whole time. The four of us took a machine each and taxied it into Number Two Hangar, and then we pulled the great sliding doors together and locked them.

The next morning, before the sun had risen from behind the mountains, a flock of Ju-87s came over and blew Number Two Hangar right off the face of the earth. Their bombing was good and they did not even hit the hangars on either side of it.

That afternoon they got Peter. He went off towards a village called Khalkis, which was being bombed by Ju-88s, and no one ever saw him again. Gay, laughing Peter, whose mother lived on a farm in Kent and who used to write to him in long, pale-blue envelopes which he carried about in his pockets.

I had always shared a tent with Peter, ever since I came to the squadron, and that evening after I had gone to bed he came back to that tent. You need not believe me; I do not expect you to, but I am telling you what happened.

I always went to bed first, because there is not room in one of those tents for two people to be turning around at the same time. Peter usually came in two or three minutes afterwards. That evening I went to bed and I lay thinking that tonight he would not be coming. I wondered whether his body lay tangled in the wreckage of his aircraft on the side of some bleak mountain or whether it was at the bottom of the sea, and I hoped only that he had had a decent funeral.

Suddenly I heard a movement. The flap of the tent opened and it shut again. But there were no footsteps. Then I heard him sit down on his bed. It was a noise that I had heard every night for weeks past and always it had been the same. It was just a thump and a creaking of the wooden legs of the camp bed. One after the other the flying boots were pulled off and dropped upon the ground, and as always one of them took three times as long to get off as the other. After that there was the gentle rustle of a blanket being pulled back and then the creakings of the rickety bed as it took the weight of a man's body.

They were sounds I had heard every night, the same sounds in the same order, and now I sat up in bed and said, 'Peter.' It was dark in the tent. My voice sounded very loud.

'Hallo, Peter. That was tough luck you had today.' But there was no answer.

I did not feel uneasy or frightened, but I remember at the time touching the tip of my nose with my finger to make sure that I was there; then because I was very tired, I went to sleep.

In the morning I looked at the bed and saw it had been slept in. But I did not show it to anyone, not even to Fin. I put the blankets back in place myself and patted the pillow.

It was on that day, 20 April 1941, that we fought the Battle of Athens. It was perhaps the last of the great dog-fighting air battles that will ever be fought, because nowadays the planes fly always in great formations of wings and squadrons, and attack is carried out methodically and scientifically upon the orders of the leader. Nowadays one does not dog-fight at all over the sky except upon very rare occasions. But the Battle of Athens was a long and beautiful dog-fight in which fifteen Hurricanes fought for half an hour with between one hundred and fifty and two hundred German bombers and fighters.

The bombers started coming over early in the afternoon. It was a lovely spring day and for the first time the sun had in it a trace of real summer warmth. The sky was blue, save for a few wispy clouds here and there and the mountains stood out black and clear against the blue of the sky.

Pentelikon no longer hid his head in the clouds. He stood over us, grim and forbidding, watching every move and knowing that each thing we did was of little purpose. Men were foolish and were made only so that they should die, while mountains and rivers went on for ever and did not notice the passing of time. Had not Pentelikon himself many years ago looked down upon Thermopylae and seen a handful of Spartans defending the pass against the invaders; seen them fight until there was not one man left alive among them? Had he not seen the Persians cut to pieces by Leonidas at Marathon, and had he not looked down upon Salamis and upon the sea when Themistocles and the Athenians drove the enemy from their shores, causing them to lose more than two hundred sail? All these things and many more he had seen, and now he looked down upon us, we were as nothing in his eyes. Almost there was a look of scorn upon the face of the mountain, and I thought for a moment that I could hear the laughter of the gods. They knew so well that we were not enough and that in the end we must lose.

The bombers came over just after lunch, and at once we saw that there were a great number of them. We looked up and saw that the sky was full of little silver specks and the sunlight danced and sparkled upon a hundred different pairs of wings.

There were fifteen Hurricanes in all and they fought like a storm in the sky. It is not easy to remember much about such a battle, but I remember looking up and seeing in the sky a mass of small black dots. I remember thinking to myself that those could not be aeroplanes; they simply could not be aeroplanes, because there were not so many aeroplanes in the world.

Then they were on us, and I remember that I applied a little flap so that I should be able to turn in tighter circles; then I remember only one or two small incidents which photographed themselves upon my mind. There were the spurts of flame from the guns of a Messerschmitt as he attacked from the frontal quarter of my starboard side. There was the German whose parachute was on fire as it opened. There was the German who flew up beside me and made rude signs at me with his fingers. There was the Hurricane which collided with a Messerschmitt. There was the aeroplane which collided with a man who was descending in a parachute, and which went into a crazy frightful spin towards the earth with the man and the parachute dangling from its port wing. There were the two bombers which collided while swerving to avoid a fighter, and I remember distinctly seeing a man being thrown clear out of the smoke and debris of the collision, hanging in mid-air with his arms outstretched and his legs apart. I tell you there was nothing that did not happen in that battle. There was the moment when I saw a single Hurricane doing tight turns around the summit of Mt Parnes with nine Messerschmitts on its tail and then I remember that suddenly the skies seemed to clear. There were no longer any aircraft in sight. The battle was over. I turned around and headed back towards Elevsis, and as I went I looked down and saw Athens and Piraeus and the rim of the sea as it curved around the gulf and travelled southward towards the Mediterranean. I saw the port of Piraeus where the bombs had fallen and I saw the smoke and fire rising above the docks. I saw the narrow coastal plain, and on it I saw tiny bonfires, thin columns of black smoke curling upward and drifting away to the east. They were the fires of aircraft which had been shot down, and I hoped only that none of them were Hurricanes.

Just then I ran straight into a Junkers 88; a straggler, the last bomber returning from the raid. He was in trouble and there was black smoke streaming from one of his engines. Although I shot at him, I don't think that it made any difference. He was coming down anyway. We were over the sea and I could tell that he wouldn't make the land. He didn't. He came down smoothly on his belly in the blue Gulf of Piraeus, two miles from the shore. I followed him and circled, waiting to make sure that the crew got out safely into their dinghy.

Slowly the machine began to sink, dipping its nose under the water and lifting its tail into the air. But there was no sign of the crew. Suddenly, without any warning, the rear gun started to fire. They opened up with their rear gun and the bullets made small jagged holes in my starboard wing. I swerved away and I remember shouting at them. I slid back the hood of the cockpit and shouted, 'You lousy brave bastards. I hope you drown.' The bomber sank soon backwards.

When I got back they were all standing around outside the hangars counting the score, and Katina was sitting on a box with tears rolling down her cheeks. But she was not crying, and Fin was kneeling down beside her, talking to her in English, quietly and gently, forgetting that she could not understand.

We lost one third of our Hurricanes in that battle, but the Germans lost more.

The Doc was dressing someone who had been burned and he looked up and said, 'You should have heard the Greeks on the aerodrome cheering as the bombers fell out of the sky.'

As we stood around talking, a truck drove up and a Greek got out and said that he had some pieces of body inside. 'This is the watch,' he said, 'that was on the arm.' It was a silver wristwatch with a luminous dial, and on the back there were some initials. We did not look inside the truck.

Now we had, I think, nine Hurricanes left.

That evening a very senior RAF officer came out from Athens and said, 'Tomorrow at dawn you will all fly to Megara. It is about ten miles down the coast. There is a small field there on which you can land. The Army is working on it throughout the night. They have two big rollers there and they are rolling it smooth. The moment you land you must hide your aircraft in the olive grove which is on the south side of the field. The ground staff are going farther south to Argos and you can join them later, but you may be able to operate from Megara for a day or two.'

Fin said, 'Where's Katina? Doc, you must find Katina and see that she gets to Argos safely.'

The Doc said, 'I will,' and we knew that we could trust him.

At dawn the next morning, when it was still dark, we took off and flew to the little field at Megara, ten miles away. We landed and hid our Hurricanes in the olive grove and broke off branches of the trees and put them over the aircraft. Then we sat down on the slope of a small hill and waited for orders.

As the sun rose up over the mountains we looked across the field and saw a mass of Greek villagers coming down from the village of Megara, coming down towards our field. There were many hundreds of them, women and children mostly, and they all came down towards our field, hurrying as they came.

Fin said, 'What the hell,' and we sat up on our little hill and watched, wondering what they were going to do.

They dispersed all around the edge of the field and gathered armfuls of heather and bracken. They carried it out on to the field, and forming themselves into long lines, they began to scatter the heather and the bracken over the grass. They were camouflaging our landing field. The rollers, when they had rolled out the ground and made it flat for landing, had left marks which were easily visible from above, and so the Greeks came out of their village, every man, woman and child, and began to put matters right. To this day I do not know who told them to do it. They stretched in a long line across the field, walking forward slowly and scattering the heather, and Fin and I went out and walked among them.

They were old women and old men mostly, very small and very sad-looking, with dark, deeply wrinkled faces, and they worked slowly scattering the heather. As we walked by, they would stop their work and smile, saying something in Greek which we could not understand. One of the children gave Fin a small pink flower and he did not know what to do with it, but walked around carrying it in his hand.

Then we went back to the slope of the hill and waited. Soon the field telephone buzzed. It was the very senior officer speaking. He said that someone must fly back to Elevsis at once and collect important messages and money. He said also that all of us must leave our little field at Megara and go to Argos that evening. The others said that they would wait until I came back with the money so that we could all fly to Argos together.

At the same time, someone had told the two Army men

who were still rolling our field to destroy their rollers so that the Germans would not get them. I remember, as I was getting into my Hurricane, seeing the two huge rollers charging towards each other across the field, and I remember seeing the Army men jump aside just before they collided. There was a great crash and I saw all the Greeks who were scattering heather stop in their work and look up. For a moment they stood rock still, looking at the rollers. Then one of them started to run. It was an old woman and she started to run back to the village as fast as she could, shouting something as she went, and instantly every man, woman and child in the field seemed to take fright and ran after her. I wanted to get out and run beside them and explain to them; to say I was sorry but that there was nothing else we could do. I wanted to tell them that we would not forget them and that one day we would come back. But it was no use. Bewildered and frightened, they ran back to their homes, and they did not stop running until they were out of sight, not even the old men.

I took off and flew to Elevsis. I landed on a dead aerodrome. There was not a soul to be seen. I parked my Hurricane, and as I walked over to the hangars the bombers came over once again. I hid in a ditch until they had finished their work, then got up and walked over to the small operations room. The telephone was still on the table, so for some reason I picked up the receiver and said, 'Hallo.'

A rather German voice at the other end answered.

I said, 'Can you hear me?' and the voice said: 'Yes, yes, I can hear you.'

'All right,' I said, 'Listen carefully.'

'Yes, continue please.'

'This is the RAF speaking. And one day we will come back, do you understand? One day we will come back.'

Then I tore the telephone from its socket and threw it through the glass of the closed window. When I went outside there was a small man in civilian clothes standing near the door. He had a revolver in one hand and a small bag in the other.

'Do you want anything?' he said in quite good English.

I said, 'Yes, I want important messages and papers which I am to carry back to Argos.'

'Here you are,' he said, as he handed me the bag. 'And good luck.'

I flew back to Megara. There were two Greek destroyers standing offshore, burning and sinking. I circled our field and the others taxied out, took off and we all flew off towards Argos.

The landing ground at Argos was just a kind of small field. It was surrounded by thick olive groves into which we taxied our aircraft for hiding. I don't know how long the field was, but it was not easy to land upon it. You had to come in low hanging on the prop, and the moment you touched down you had to start putting on the brake, jerking it on and jerking it off again the moment she started to nose over. But only one man overshot and crashed.

The ground staff had arrived already and as we got out of our aircraft Katina came running up with a basket of black olives, offering them to us and pointing to our stomachs, indicating that we must eat.

Fin bent down and ruffled her hair with his hand. He said, 'Katina, one day we must go into town and buy you a new dress.' She smiled at him but did not understand and we all started to eat black olives.

Then I looked around and saw that the wood was full of aircraft. Around every corner there was an aeroplane hidden in the trees, and when we asked about it we learned that the Greeks had brought the whole of their air force down to Argos and parked them in that little wood. They were peculiar ancient models, not one of them less than five years old, and I don't know how many dozen there were there.

That night we slept under the trees. We wrapped Katina up in a large flying suit and gave her a flying helmet for a pillow, and after she had gone to sleep we sat around eating black olives and drinking resinato out of an enormous cask. But we were very tired, and soon we fell asleep.

All the next day we saw the truckloads of troops moving down the road towards the sea, and as often as we could we took off and flew above them.

The Germans kept coming over and bombing the road near by, but they had not yet spotted our airfield.

Later in the day we were told that every available Hurricane was to take off at six p.m. to protect an important shipping move, and the nine machines, which were all that were now left, were refuelled and got ready. At three minutes to six we began to taxi out of the olive grove on to the field.

The first two machines took off, but just as they left the ground something black swept down out of the sky and shot them both down in flames. I looked around and saw at least fifty Messerschmitt 110s circling our field, and even as I looked some of them turned and came down upon the remaining seven Hurricanes which were waiting to take off.

There was no time to do anything. Each one of our aircraft was hit in that first swoop, although funnily enough only one of the pilots was hurt. It was impossible now to take off, so we jumped out of our aircraft, hauled the wounded pilot out of his cockpit and ran with him back to the slit trenches, to the wonderful big, deep zigzagging slit trenches which had been dug by the Greeks.

The Messerschmitts took their time. There was no opposition either from the ground or from the air, except that Fin was firing his revolver.

It is not a pleasant thing to be ground-strafed, especially if they have cannon in their wings; and unless one has a deep slit trench in which to lie, there is no future in it. For some reason, perhaps because they thought it was a good joke, the German pilots went for the slit trenches before they bothered about the aircraft. The first ten minutes was spent rushing madly around the corners of the trenches so as not to be caught in a trench which ran parallel with the line of flight of the attacking aircraft. It was a hectic, dreadful ten minutes, with everyone shouting, 'Here comes another,' and scrambling and rushing to get around the corner into the other section of the trench.

Then the Germans went for the Hurricanes and at the same time for the mass of old Greek aircraft parked all around the olive grove, and one by one, methodically and systematically, they set them on fire. The noise was terrific, and everywhere – in the trees, on the rocks and on the grass – the bullets splattered.

I remember peeping cautiously over the top of our trench and seeing a small white flower growing just a few inches away from my nose. It was pure white and it had three petals. I remember looking past it and seeing three of the Germans diving on my own Hurricane which was parked on the other side of the field and I remember shouting at them, although I do not know what I said.

Then suddenly I saw Katina. She was running out from the far corner of the aerodrome, running right out into the middle of this mass of blazing guns and burning aircraft, running as fast as she could. Once she stumbled, but she scrambled to her feet again and went on running. Then she stopped and stood looking up, raising her fists at the planes as they flew past.

Now as she stood there, I remember seeing one of the Messerschmitts turning and coming in low straight towards her and I remember thinking that she was so small that she could not be hit. I remember seeing the spurts of flame from his guns as he came, and I remember seeing the child, for a split second, standing quite still, facing the machine. I remember that the wind was blowing in her hair.

Then she was down.

The next moment I shall never forget. On every side, as if by magic, men appeared out of the ground. They swarmed out of their trenches and like a crazy mob poured on to the aerodrome, running towards the tiny little bundle which lay motionless in the middle of the field. They ran fast, crouching as they went, and I remember jumping up out of my slit trench and joining with them. I remember thinking of nothing at all and watching the boots of the man in front of me, noticing that he was a little bow-legged and that his blue trousers were much too long.

I remember seeing Fin arrive first, followed closely by a sergeant called Wishful, and I remember seeing the two of them pick up Katina and start running with her back towards the trenches. I saw her leg, which was just a lot of blood and bones, and I saw her chest where the blood was spurting out on to her white print dress; I saw, for a moment, her face, which was white as the snow on top of Olympus.

I ran beside Fin, and as he ran, he kept saying, 'The lousy bastards, the lousy, bloody bastards'; and then as we got to our trench I remember looking round and finding that there was no longer any noise or shooting. The Germans had gone.

Fin said, 'Where's the Doc?' and suddenly there he was, standing beside us, looking at Katina – looking at her face.

The Doc gently touched her wrist and without looking up he said, 'She is not alive.'

They put her down under a little tree, and when I turned away I saw on all sides the fires of countless burning aircraft. I saw my own Hurricane burning near by and I stood staring hopelessly into the flames as they danced around the engine and licked against the metal of the wings.

I stood staring into the flames, and as I stared, the fire became a deeper red and I saw beyond it not a tangled mass of smoking wreckage, but the flames of a hotter and intenser fire which now burned and smouldered in the hearts of the people of Greece.

Still I stared, and as I stared I saw in the centre of the fire, whence the red flames sprang, a bright, white heat, shining bright and without any colour.

As I stared, the brightness diffused and became soft and yellow like sunlight, and through it, beyond it, I saw a young child standing in the middle of a field with the sunlight shining in her hair. For a moment she stood looking up into the sky, which was clear and blue and without any clouds; then she turned and looked towards me, and as she turned I saw that the front of her white print dress was stained deep red, the colour of blood.

Then there was no longer any fire or any flames and I saw before me only the glowing twisted wreckage of a burned-out plane. I must have been standing there for quite a long time.

The Sound Machine

First published in *The New Yorker*
(17 September 1949)

It was a warm summer evening and Klausner walked quickly through the front gate and around the side of the house and into the garden at the back. He went on down the garden until he came to a wooden shed and he unlocked the door, went inside and closed the door behind him.

The interior of the shed was an unpainted room. Against one wall, on the left, there was a long wooden workbench, and on it, among a littering of wires and batteries and small sharp tools, there stood a black box about three feet long, the shape of a child's coffin.

Klausner moved across the room to the box. The top of the box was open, and he bent down and began to poke and peer inside it among a mass of different-coloured wires and silver tubes. He picked up a piece of paper that lay beside the box, studied it carefully, put it down, peered inside the box and started running his fingers along the wires, tugging gently at them to test the connections, glancing back at the paper, then into the box, then at the paper again, checking each wire. He did this for perhaps an hour.

Then he put a hand around to the front of the box where there were three dials, and he began to twiddle them, watching at the same time the movement of the mechanism inside the box. All the while he kept speaking softly to himself, nodding his head, smiling sometimes, his hands always moving, the fingers moving swiftly, deftly, inside the box, his mouth twisting into curious shapes when a thing was delicate or difficult to do, saying, 'Yes ... Yes ... And now this one ... Yes ... Yes ... But is this right? Is it – where's my diagram? ... Ah, yes ... Of course ... Yes, yes ... That's right ... And now ... Good ... Good ... Yes ... Yes, yes, yes.' His concentration was intense; his movements were quick; there was an air of urgency about the way he worked, of breathlessness, of strong suppressed excitement.

Suddenly he heard footsteps on the gravel path outside and he straightened and turned swiftly as the door opened and a tall man came in. It was Scott. It was only Scott, the doctor.

'Well, well, well,' the doctor said. 'So this is where you hide yourself in the evenings.'

'Hullo, Scott,' Klausner said.

'I happened to be passing,' the doctor told him, 'so I dropped in to see how you were. There was no one in the house, so I came on down here. How's that throat of yours been behaving?'

'It's all right. It's fine.'

'Now I'm here I might as well have a look at it.'

'Please don't trouble. I'm quite cured. I'm fine.'

The doctor began to feel the tension in the room. He looked at the black box on the bench; then he looked at the man. 'You've got your hat on,' he said.

'Oh, have I?' Klausner reached up, removed the hat and put it on the bench.

The doctor came up closer and bent down to look into the box. 'What's this?' he said. 'Making a radio?'

'No. Just fooling around.'

'It's got rather complicated-looking innards.'

'Yes.' Klausner seemed tense and distracted.

'What is it?' the doctor asked. 'It's rather a frightening-looking thing, isn't it?'

'It's just an idea.'

'Yes?'

'It has to do with sound, that's all.'

'Good heavens, man! Don't you get enough of that sort of thing all day in your work?'

'I like sound.'

'So it seems.' The doctor went to the door, turned, and said, 'Well, I won't disturb you. Glad your throat's not worrying you any more.' But he kept standing there, looking at the box, intrigued by the remarkable complexity of its inside, curious to know what this strange patient of his was up to. 'What's it really for?' he asked. 'You've made me inquisitive.'

Klausner looked down at the box, then at the doctor, and he reached up and began gently to scratch the lobe of his right ear. There was a pause. The doctor stood by the door, waiting, smiling.

'All right, I'll tell you, if you're interested.' There was another pause, and the doctor could see that Klausner was having trouble about how to begin.

He was shifting from one foot to the other, tugging at the lobe of his ear, looking at his feet, and then at last, slowly, he said, 'Well, it's like this . . . the theory is very

64

simple, really. The human ear . . . You know that it can't hear everything. There are sounds that are so low-pitched or so high-pitched that it can't hear them.'

'Yes,' the doctor said. 'Yes.'

'Well, speaking very roughly, any note so high that it has more than fifteen thousand vibrations a second – we can't hear it. Dogs have better ears than us. You know you can buy a whistle whose note is so high-pitched that you can't hear it at all. But a dog can hear it.'

'Yes, I've seen one,' the doctor said.

'Of course you have. And up the scale, higher than the note of that whistle, there is another note – a vibration if you like, but I prefer to think of it as a note. You can't hear that one either. And above that there is another and another rising right up the scale for ever and ever and ever, an endless succession of notes . . . an infinity of notes . . . there is a note – if only our ears could hear it – so high that it vibrates a million times a second . . . and another a million times as high as that . . . and on and on, higher and higher, as far as numbers go, which is . . . infinity . . . eternity . . . beyond the stars.'

Klausner was becoming more animated every moment. He was a small frail man, nervous and twitchy, with always-moving hands. His large head inclined towards his left shoulder as though his neck were not quite strong enough to support it rigidly. His face was smooth and pale, almost white, and the pale-grey eyes that blinked and peered from behind a pair of steel spectacles were bewildered, unfocused, remote. He was a frail, nervous, twitchy little man, a moth of a man, dreamy and distracted; suddenly fluttering and animated; and now the doctor, looking at that strange pale face and those pale-grey eyes, felt that somehow there was about this little person a quality of distance, of immense, immeasurable distance, as though the mind were far away from where the body was.

The doctor waited for him to go on. Klausner sighed and clasped his hands tightly together. 'I believe,' he said, speaking more slowly now, 'that there is a whole world of sound about us all the time that we cannot hear. It is possible that up there in those high-pitched inaudible regions there is a new exciting music being made, with subtle harmonies and fierce grinding discords, a music so powerful that it would drive us mad if only our ears were tuned to hear the sound of it. There may be anything . . . for all we know there may –'

'Yes,' the doctor said. 'But it's not very probable.'

'Why not? Why not?' Klausner pointed to a fly sitting on a small roll of copper wire on the workbench. 'You see that fly? What sort of a noise is that fly making now? None – that one can hear. But for all we know the creature may be whistling like mad on a very high note, or barking or croaking or singing a song. It's got a mouth, hasn't it? It's got a throat!'

The doctor looked at the fly and he smiled. He was still standing by the door with his hand on the doorknob. 'Well,' he said. 'So you're going to check up on that?'

'Some time ago,' Klausner said, 'I made a simple instrument that proved to me the existence of many odd inaudible sounds. Often I have sat and watched the needle of my instrument recording the presence of sound vibrations in the air when I myself could hear nothing. And *those* are the sounds I want to listen to. I want to know where they come from and who or what is making them.'

'And that machine on the table there,' the doctor said, 'is that going to allow you to hear these noises?'

'It may. Who knows? So far, I've had no luck. But I've made some changes in it and tonight I'm ready for another trial. This machine,' he said, touching it with his hands, 'is designed to pick up sound vibrations that are too high-pitched for reception by the human ear, and to convert them to a scale of audible tones. I tune it in, almost like a radio.'

'How d' you mean?'

'It isn't complicated. Say I wish to listen to the squeak of a bat. That's a fairly high-pitched sound – about thirty thousand vibrations a second. The average human ear can't quite hear it. Now, if there were a bat flying around this room and I tuned in to thirty thousand on my machine, I would hear the squeaking of that bat very clearly. I would even hear the correct note – F sharp, or B flat, or what-ever it might be – but merely at a much *lower pitch*. Don't you understand?'

The doctor looked at the long black coffin-box. 'And you're going to try it tonight?'

'Yes.'

'Well, I wish you luck.' He glanced at his watch. 'My goodness!' he said. 'I must fly. Good-bye, and thank you for telling me. I must call again some time and find out what happened.' The doctor went out and closed the door behind him.

For a while longer, Klausner fussed about with the wires in the black box; then he straightened up and in a soft excited whisper said, 'Now we'll try again . . . We'll take it out into the garden this time . . . and then perhaps . . . perhaps . . . the reception will be better. Lift it up now . . . carefully . . . Oh, my God, it's heavy!' He carried the box to the door, found that he couldn't open the door without putting it down, carried it back, put it on the bench, opened the door, and then carried it with some difficulty into the garden. He placed the box carefully on a small wooden table that stood on the lawn. He returned to the shed and fetched a pair of earphones. He plugged the wire connections from the earphones into the machine and put the earphones over his ears. The movements of his hands were quick and precise. He was excited, and breathed loudly and quickly through his mouth. He kept on talking to himself with little words of comfort and encouragement, as though he were afraid – afraid that the machine might not work and afraid also of what might happen if it did.

He stood there in the garden beside the wooden table, so pale, small and thin that he looked like an ancient, consumptive, bespectacled child. The sun had gone down. There was no wind, no sound at all. From where he stood, he could see over a low fence into the next garden, and there was a woman walking down the garden with a flower basket on her arm. He watched her for a while without thinking about her at all. Then he turned to the box on the table and pressed a switch on its front. He put his left hand on the volume control and his right on the knob that moved a needle across a large central dial, like the wave-length dial of a radio. The dial was marked with many numbers, in a series of bands, starting at fifteen thousand and going on up to one million.

And now he was bending forward over the machine. His head was cocked to one side in a tense listening atti-tude. His right hand was beginning to turn the knob. The needle was travelling slowly across the dial, so slowly he could hardly see it move, and in the earphones he could hear a faint, spasmodic crackling.

Behind this crackling sound he could hear a distant humming tone which was the noise of the machine itself, but that was all. As he listened, he became conscious of a curious sensation, a feeling that his ears were stretching out away from his head, that each ear was connected to his head by a thin stiff wire, like a tentacle, and that the wires were lengthening, that the ears were going up and up towards a secret and forbidden territory, a dangerous ultrasonic region where ears had never been before and had no right to be.

The little needle crept slowly across the dial, and sud-denly he heard a shriek, a frightful piercing shriek, and he jumped and dropped his hands, catching hold of the edge of the table. He stared around him as if expecting to see the person who had shrieked. There was no one in sight except the woman in the garden next door, and it was cer-tainly not she. She was bending down, cutting yellow roses and putting them in her basket.

Again it came – a throatless, inhuman shriek, sharp and short, very clear and cold. The note itself possessed a minor, metallic quality that he had never heard before. Klausner looked around him, searching instinctively for the source of the noise. The woman next door was the only living thing in sight. He saw her reach down, take a rose stem in the fingers of one hand and snip the stem with a pair of scissors. Again he heard the scream.

It came at the exact moment when the rose stem was cut.

At this point, the woman straightened up, put the scissors in the basket with the roses and turned to walk away.

'Mrs Saunders!' Klausner shouted, his voice shrill with excitement. 'Oh, Mrs Saunders!'

And looking round, the woman saw her neighbour standing on his lawn – a fantastic, arm-waving little person with a pair of earphones on his head – calling to her in a voice so high and loud that she became alarmed.

'Cut another one! Please cut another one quickly!'

She stood still, staring at him. 'Why, Mr Klausner,' she said, 'what's the matter?'

'Please do as I ask,' he said. 'Cut just one more rose!'

Mrs Saunders had always believed her neighbour to be a rather peculiar person; now it seemed that he had gone completely crazy. She wondered whether she should run into the house and fetch her husband. No, she thought. No, he's harmless. I'll just humour him. 'Certainly, Mr Klausner, if you like,' she said. She took her scissors from the basket, bent down and snipped another rose.

Again Klausner heard that frightful, throatless shriek in the earphones; again it came at the exact moment the rose stem was cut. He took off the earphones and ran to the fence that separated the two gardens. 'All right,' he said. 'That's enough. No more. Please, no more.'

The woman stood there, a yellow rose in one hand, clippers in the other, looking at him.

'I'm going to tell you something, Mrs Saunders,' he said, 'something that you won't believe.' He put his hands on top of the fence and peered at her intently through his thick spectacles. 'You have, this evening, cut a basketful of roses. You have with a sharp pair of scissors cut through the stems of living things, and each rose that you cut screamed in the most terrible way. Did you know that, Mrs Saunders?'

'No,' she said. 'I certainly didn't know that.'

'It happens to be true,' he said. He was breathing rather rapidly, but he was trying to control his excitement. 'I heard them shrieking. Each time you cut one, I heard the cry of pain. A very high-pitched sound, approximately one hundred and thirty-two thousand vibrations a second. You couldn't possibly have heard it yourself. But *I* heard it.'

'Did you really, Mr Klausner?' She decided she would make a dash for the house in about five seconds.

'You might say,' he went on, 'that a rosebush has no nervous system to feel with, no throat to cry with. You'd be right. It hasn't. Not like ours, anyway. But *how do you know, Mrs Saunders*' – and here he leaned far over the fence and spoke in a fierce whisper – '*how do you know* that a rosebush doesn't feel as much pain when someone cuts its stem in two as you would feel if someone cut your wrist off with a garden shears? *How do you know that?* It's *alive*, isn't it?'

'Yes, Mr Klausner. Oh yes – and good night.' Quickly she turned and ran up the garden to her house. Klausner went back to the table. He put on the earphones and stood for a while listening. He could still hear the faint crackling sound and the humming noise of the machine, but nothing more. He bent down and took hold of a small white daisy growing on the lawn. He took it between thumb and forefinger and slowly pulled it upwards and sideways until the stem broke.

From the moment that he started pulling to the moment when the stem broke, he heard – he distinctly heard in the earphones – a faint high-pitched cry, curiously inanimate. He took another daisy and did it again. Once more he heard the cry, but he wasn't so sure now that it expressed *pain*. No, it wasn't pain; it was surprise. Or was it? It didn't really express any of the feelings or emotions known to a human being. It was just a cry, a neutral, stony cry – a single emotionless note, expressing nothing. It had been the same with the roses. He had been wrong in calling it a cry of pain. A flower probably didn't feel pain. It felt something else which we didn't know about – something called toin or spurl or plinuckment, or anything you like.

He stood up and removed the earphones. It was getting dark and he could see pricks of light shining in the windows of the houses all around him. Carefully he picked up the black box from the table, carried it into the shed and put it on the workbench. Then he went out, locked the door behind him and walked up to the house.

The next morning Klausner was up as soon as it was light. He dressed and went straight to the shed. He picked up the machine and carried it outside, clasping it to his chest with both hands, walking unsteadily under its weight. He went past the house, out through the front gate, and across the road to the park. There he paused and looked around him; then he went on until he came to a large tree, a beech tree, and he placed the machine on the ground close to the trunk of the tree. Quickly he went back to the house and got an axe from the coal cellar and carried it across the road into the park. He put the axe on the ground beside the tree.

Then he looked around him again, peering nervously through his thick glasses in every direction. There was no one about. It was six in the morning.

He put the earphones on his head and switched on the machine. He listened for a moment to the faint familiar humming sound; then he picked up the axe, took a stance with his legs wide apart and swung the axe as hard as he could at the base of the tree-trunk. The blade cut deep into the wood and stuck there, and at the instant of impact he heard a most extraordinary noise in the earphones. It was a new noise, unlike any he had heard before – a harsh, noteless, enormous noise, a growling, low-pitched, scream-ing sound, not quick and short like the noise of the roses, but drawn out like a sob, lasting for fully a minute, loudest at the moment when the axe struck, fading gradually fainter and fainter until it was gone.

Klausner stared in horror at the place where the blade of the axe had sunk into the woodflesh of the tree; then gently he took the axe handle, worked the blade loose and threw the thing on the ground. With his fingers he touched the gash that the axe had made in the wood, touching the edges of the gash, trying to press them together to close the wound, and he kept saying, 'Tree . . . oh tree . . . I am sorry . . . I am so sorry . . . but it will heal . . . it will heal fine . . .'

For a while he stood there with his hands upon the trunk of the great tree; then suddenly he turned away and hurried off out of the park, across the road, through the front gate and back into his house. He went to the telephone, consulted the book, dialled a number and waited. He held the receiver tightly in his left hand and tapped the table impatiently with his right. He heard the telephone buzzing at the other end, and then the click of a lifted receiver and a man's voice, a sleepy voice, saying: 'Hullo. Yes.'

'Dr Scott?' he said.

'Yes. Speaking.'

'Dr Scott. You must come at once – quickly please.'

'Who is it speaking?'

'Klausner here, and you remember what I told you last night about my experiment with sound, and how I hoped I might –'

'Yes, yes, of course, but what's the matter? Are you ill?'

'No, I'm not ill, but –'

'It's half past six in the morning,' the doctor said, 'and you call me, but you are not ill.'

'Please come. Come quickly. I want someone to hear it. It's driving me mad! I can't believe it . . .'

The doctor heard the frantic, almost hysterical note in the man's voice, the same note he was used to hearing in the voices of the people who called up and said, 'There's been an accident. Come quickly.' He said slowly, 'You really want me to get out of bed and come over now?'

'Yes, now. At once please.'

'All right then, I'll come.'

Klausner sat down beside the telephone and waited. He tried to remember what the shriek of the tree had sounded like, but he couldn't. He could remember only that it had been enormous and frightful and that it had made him feel sick with horror. He tried to imagine what sort of a noise a human would make if he had to stand anchored to the ground while someone deliberately swung a small sharp thing at his leg so that the blade cut in deep and wedged itself in the cut. Same sort of noise perhaps? No. Quite different. The noise of the tree was worse than any known human noise because of that frightening, toneless, throatless quality. He began to wonder about other living things, and he thought immediately of a field of wheat, a field of wheat standing up straight and yellow and alive, with the mower going through it, cutting the stems, five hundred stems a second, every second. Oh, my God, what would *that* noise be like? Five hundred wheat plants screaming together, and every second another five hundred being cut and screaming and – no, he thought, I do not want to go to a wheat field with my machine. I would never eat bread after that. But what about potatoes and cabbages and carrots and onions? And what about apples? Ah, no. Apples are all right. They fall off naturally when they are ripe. Apples are all right if you let them fall off instead of tearing them from the tree branch. But not vegetables. Not a potato for example. A potato would surely shriek; so would a carrot and an onion and a cabbage . . .

He heard the click of the front-gate latch and he jumped up and went out and saw the tall doctor coming down the path, little black bag in hand.

'Well,' the doctor said. 'Well, what's all the trouble?'

'Come with me, Doctor. I want you to hear it. I called you because you're the only one I've told. It's over the road in the park. Will you come now?'

The doctor looked at him. He seemed calmer now. There was no sign of madness or hysteria; he was merely disturbed and excited.

They went across the road into the park and Klausner led the way to the great beech tree at the foot of which stood the long black coffin-box of the machine – and the axe.

'Why did you bring it out here?' the doctor asked.

'I wanted a tree. There aren't any big trees in the garden.'

'And why the axe?'

'You'll see in a moment. But now please put on these earphones and listen. Listen carefully and tell me afterwards precisely what you hear. I want to make quite sure . . .'

The doctor smiled and took the earphones and put them over his ears.

Klausner bent down and flicked the switch on the panel of the machine; then he picked up the axe and took his stance with his legs apart, ready to swing. For a moment he paused. 'Can you hear anything?' he said to the doctor.

'Can I what?'

'Can you *hear* anything?'

'Just a humming noise.'

Klausner stood there with the axe in his hands trying to bring himself to swing, but the thought of the noise that the tree would make made him pause again.

'What are you waiting for?' the doctor asked.

'Nothing,' Klausner answered, and then he lifted the axe and swung it at the tree; and as he swung, he thought he felt, he could swear he felt a movement of the ground on which he stood. He felt a slight shifting of the earth beneath his feet as though the roots of the tree were moving underneath the soil, but it was too late to check the blow and the axe blade struck the tree and wedged deep into the wood. At that moment, high overhead, there was the cracking sound of wood splintering and the swishing sound of leaves brushing against other leaves and they both looked up and the doctor cried, 'Watch out! Run, man! Quickly, run!'

The doctor had ripped off the earphones and was running away fast, but Klausner stood spellbound, staring up at the great branch, sixty feet long at least, that was bending slowly downwards, breaking and crackling and splintering at its thickest point, where it joined the main trunk of the tree. The branch came crashing down and Klausner leaped aside just in time. It fell upon the machine and smashed it into pieces.

'Great heavens!' shouted the doctor as he came running back. 'That was a near one! I thought it had got you!'

Klausner was staring at the tree. His large head was

leaning to one side and upon his smooth white face there was a tense, horrified expression. Slowly he walked up to the tree and gently he prised the blade loose from the trunk.

'Did you hear it?' he said, turning to the doctor. His voice was barely audible.

The doctor was still out of breath from the running and the excitement. 'Hear what?'

'In the earphones. Did you hear anything when the axe struck?'

The doctor began to rub the back of his neck. 'Well,' he said, 'as a matter of fact . . .' He paused and frowned and bit his lower lip. 'No, I'm not sure. I couldn't be sure. I don't suppose I had the earphones on for more than a second after the axe struck.'

'Yes, yes, but what did you hear?'

'I don't know,' the doctor said. 'I don't know what I heard. Probably the noise of the branch breaking.' He was speaking rapidly, rather irritably.

'What did it sound like?' Klausner leaned forward slightly, staring hard at the doctor. '*Exactly* what did it sound like?'

'Oh hell!' the doctor said. 'I really don't know. I was more interested in getting out of the way. Let's leave it.'

'Dr Scott, *what-did-it-sound-like?*'

'For God's sake, how could I tell, what with half the tree falling on me and having to run for my life?' The doctor certainly seemed nervous. Klausner had sensed it now. He stood quite still, staring at the doctor, and for fully half a minute he didn't speak. The doctor moved his feet, shrugged his shoulders and half turned to go. 'Well,' he said. 'We'd better get back.'

'Look,' said the little man, and now his smooth white face became suddenly suffused with colour. 'Look,' he said, 'you stitch this up.' He pointed to the last gash that the axe had made in the tree-trunk. 'You stitch this up quickly.'

'Don't be silly,' the doctor said.

'You do as I say. Stitch it up.' Klausner was gripping the axe handle and he spoke softly, in a curious, almost a threatening tone.

'Don't be silly,' the doctor said. 'I can't stitch through wood. Come on. Let's get back.'

'So you can't stitch through wood?'

'No, of course not.'

'Have you got any iodine in your bag?'

'What if I have?'

'Then paint the cut with iodine. It'll sting, but that can't be helped.'

'Now look,' the doctor said, and again he turned as if to go. 'Let's not be ridiculous. Let's get back to the house and then . . .'

'*Paint-the-cut-with-iodine.*'

The doctor hesitated. He saw Klausner's hands tightening on the handle of the axe. He decided that his only alternative was to run away fast, and he certainly wasn't going to do that.

'All right,' he said. 'I'll paint it with iodine.'

He got his black bag, which was lying on the grass about ten yards away, opened it and took out a bottle of iodine and some cotton-wool. He went up to the tree-trunk, uncorked the bottle, tipped some of the iodine on to the cotton-wool, bent down and began to dab it into the cut. He kept one eye on Klausner who was standing motionless with the axe in his hands, watching him.

'Make sure you get it right in.'

'Yes,' the doctor said.

'Now do the other one, the one just above it!'

The doctor did as he was told.

'There you are,' he said. 'It's done.'

He straightened up and surveyed his work in a very serious manner. 'That should do nicely.'

Klausner came closer and gravely examined the two wounds.

'Yes,' he said, nodding his huge head slowly up and down. 'Yes, that will do nicely.' He stepped back a pace. 'You'll come and look at them again tomorrow?'

'Oh yes,' the doctor said. 'Of course.'

'And put some more iodine on?'

'If necessary, yes.'

'Thank you, Doctor,' Klausner said, and he nodded his head again and dropped the axe and all at once he smiled, a wild excited smile, and quickly the doctor went over to him and gently he took him by the arm and he said, 'Come on, we must go now,' and suddenly they were walking away, the two of them, walking silently, rather hurriedly, across the park, over the road, back to the house.

An African Story

First published in *Over to You* (1945)

For England, the war began in September 1939. The people on the island knew about it at once and began to prepare themselves. In farther places the people heard about it a few minutes afterwards, and they too began to prepare themselves.

And in East Africa, in Kenya Colony, there was a young man who was a white hunter, who loved the plains and the valleys and the cool nights on the slopes of Kilimanjaro. He too heard about the war and began to prepare himself. He made his way over the country to Nairobi, and he reported to the RAF and asked that they make him a pilot. They took him in and he began his training at Nairobi Airport, flying in little Tiger Moths and doing well with his flying.

After five weeks he nearly got court-martialled because he took his plane up and instead of practising spins and stall-turns as he had been ordered to do, he flew off in the direction of Nakuru to look at the wild animals on the plain. On the way, he thought he saw a Sable antelope, and because these are rare animals, he became excited and flew down low to get a better view. He was looking down at the antelope out of the left side of the cockpit, and because of this he did not see the giraffe on the other side. The leading edge of the starboard wing struck the neck of the giraffe just below the head and cut clean through it. He was flying as low as that. There was damage to the wing, but he managed to get back to Nairobi, and as I said, he was nearly court-martialled, because you cannot explain away a thing like that by saying you hit a large bird, not when there are pieces of giraffe skin and giraffe hair sticking to the wing and the stays.

After six weeks he was allowed to make his first solo cross-country flight, and he flew off from Nairobi to a place called Eldoret, which is a little town eight thousand feet up in the Highlands. But again he was unlucky. This time he had engine failure on the way, due to water in the fuel tanks. He kept his head and made a beautiful forced landing without damaging the aircraft, not far from a little shack which stood alone on the highland plain with no other habitation in sight. That is lonely country up there.

He walked over to the shack, and there he found an old man, living alone, with nothing but a small patch of sweet potatoes, some brown chickens and a black cow.

The old man was kind to him. He gave him food and milk and a place to sleep, and the pilot stayed with him for two days and two nights, until a rescue plane from Nairobi spotted his aircraft on the ground, landed beside it, found out what was wrong, went away and came back with clean petrol which enabled him to take off and return.

But during his stay, the old man, who was lonely and had seen no one for many months, was glad of his company and of the opportunity to talk. He talked much and the pilot listened. He talked of the lonely life, of the lions that came in the night, of the rogue elephant that lived over the hill in the west, of the hotness of the days and of the silence that came with the cold at midnight.

On the second night he talked about himself. He told a long, strange story, and as he told it, it seemed to the pilot that the old man was lifting a great weight off his shoulders in the telling. When he had finished, he said that he had never told that to anyone before, and that he would never tell it to anyone again, but the story was so strange that the pilot wrote it down on paper as soon as he got back to Nairobi. He wrote it not in the old man's words, but in his own words, painting it as a picture with the old man as a character in the picture, because that was the best way to do it. He had never written a story before, and so naturally there were mistakes. He did not know any of the tricks with words which writers use, which they have to use just as painters have to use tricks with paint, but when he had finished writing, when he put down his pencil and went over to the airmen's canteen for a pint of beer, he left behind him a rare and powerful tale.

We found it in his suitcase two weeks later when we were going through his belongings after he had been killed in training, and because he seemed to have no relatives, and because he was my friend, I took the manuscript and looked after it for him.

This is what he wrote.

The old man came out of the door into the bright sunshine, and for a moment he stood leaning on his stick, looking around him, blinking at the strong light. He stood with his head on one side, looking up, listening for the noise which he thought he had heard.

He was small and thick and well over seventy years old, although he looked nearer eighty-five, because rheumatism had tied his body into knots. His face was covered with grey hair, and when he moved his mouth, he moved it only on one side of his face. On his head, whether indoors or out, he wore a dirty white topee.

He stood quite still in the bright sunshine, screwing up his eyes, listening for the noise.

Yes, there it was again. The head of the old man flicked around and he looked towards the small wooden hut standing a hundred yards away on the pasture. This time there was no doubt about it: the yelp of a dog, the high-pitched, sharp-piercing yelp of pain which a dog gives when he is in great danger. Twice more it came and this time the noise was more like a scream than a yelp. The note was higher and more sharp, as though it were wrenched quickly from some small place inside the body.

The old man turned and limped fast across the grass towards the wooden shed where Judson lived, pushed open the door and went in.

The small white dog was lying on the floor and Judson was standing over it, his legs apart, his black hair falling all over his long, red face; standing there tall and skinny, muttering to himself and sweating through his greasy white shirt. His mouth hung open in an odd way, a lifeless way, as though his jaw was too heavy for him, and he was dribbling gently down the middle of his chin. He stood there looking at the small white dog which was lying on the floor, and with one hand he was slowly twisting his left ear; in the other he held a heavy bamboo.

The old man ignored Judson and went down on his knees beside his dog, gently running his thin hands over its body. The dog lay still, looking up at him with watery eyes. Judson did not move. He was watching the dog and the man.

Slowly the old man got up, rising with difficulty, holding the top of his stick with both hands and pulling himself to his feet. He looked around the room. There was a dirty rumpled mattress lying on the floor in the far corner; there was a wooden table made of packing cases and on it a Primus stove and a chipped blue-enamelled saucepan. There were chicken feathers and mud on the floor.

The old man saw what he wanted. It was a heavy iron bar standing against the wall near the mattress, and he hobbled over towards it, thumping the hollow wooden floorboards with his stick as he went. The eyes of the dog followed his movements as he limped across the room. The old man changed his stick to his left hand, took the iron bar in his right, hobbled back to the dog and, without pausing, he lifted the bar and brought it down hard upon the animal's head. He threw the bar to the ground and looked up at Judson, who was standing there with his legs apart, dribbling down his chin and twitching around the corners of his eyes. He went right up to him and began to speak. He spoke very quietly and slowly, with a terrible anger, and as he spoke he moved only one side of his mouth.

'You killed him,' he said. 'You broke his back.'

Then, as the tide of anger rose and gave him strength, he found more words. He looked up and spat them into the face of the tall Judson, who twitched around the corners of his eyes and backed away towards the wall.

'You lousy, mean, dog-beating bastard. That was my dog. What the hell right have you got beating my dog, tell me that. Answer me, you slobbering madman. Answer me.'

Judson was slowly rubbing the palm of his left hand up and down on the front of his shirt, and now the whole of his face began to twitch. Without looking up, he said, 'He wouldn't stop licking that old place on his paw. I couldn't stand the noise it made. You know I can't stand noises like that, licking, licking, licking. I told him to stop. He looked up and wagged his tail; but then he went on licking. I couldn't stand it any longer, so I beat him.'

The old man did not say anything. For a moment it looked as though he were going to hit this creature. He half raised his arm, dropped it again, spat on the floor, turned around and hobbled out of the door into the sunshine. He went across the grass to where a black cow was standing in the shade of a small acacia tree, chewing its cud, and the cow watched him as he came limping across the grass from the shed. But it went on chewing, munching its cud, moving its jaws regularly, mechanically, like a metronome in slow time. The old man came limping up and stood beside it, stroking its neck. Then he leaned against its shoulder and scratched its back with the butt-end of his stick. He stood there for a long time, leaning against the cow, scratching it with his stick; and now and again he would speak to it, speaking quiet little words, whispering them almost, like a person telling a secret to another.

It was shady under the acacia tree, and the country around him looked lush and pleasant after the long rains, for the grass grows green up in the Highlands of Kenya; and at this time of year, after the rains, it is as green and rich as any grass in the world. Away in the north stood Mount Kenya itself, with snow upon its head, with a thin white plume trailing from its summit where the icy winds made a storm and blew the white powder from the top of the mountain. Down below, upon the slopes of that same mountain there were lion and elephant, and sometimes during the night one could hear the roar of the lions as they looked at the moon.

The days passed and Judson went about his work on the farm in a silent, mechanical kind of way, taking in the corn, digging the sweet potatoes and milking the black cow, while the old man stayed indoors away from the fierce African sun. Only in the late afternoon when the air began to get cool and sharp did he hobble outside, and always he went over to his black cow and spent an hour with it under the acacia tree. One day when he came out he found Judson standing beside the cow, regarding it strangely, standing in a peculiar attitude with one foot in front of the other and gently twisting his ear with his right hand.

'What is it now?' said the old man as he came limping up.

'Cow won't stop chewing,' said Judson.

'Chewing her cud,' said the old man. 'Leave her alone.'

Judson said, 'It's the noise, can't you hear it? Crunchy noise like she was chewing pebbles, only she isn't; she's chewing grass and spit. Look at her, she goes on and on crunching, crunching, crunching, and it's just grass and spit. Noise goes right into my head.'

'Get out,' said the old man. 'Get out of my sight.'

At dawn the old man sat, as he always did, looking out of his window, watching Judson coming across from his hut to milk the cow. He saw him coming sleepily across the field, talking to himself as he walked, dragging his feet, making a dark-green trail in the wet grass, carrying in his hand the old four-gallon kerosene tin which he used as a milk pail. The sun was coming up over the escarpment and making long shadows behind the man, the cow and the little acacia tree. The old man saw Judson put down the tin and he saw him fetch the box from beside the acacia tree and settle himself upon it, ready for the milking. He saw him suddenly kneeling down, feeling the udder of the cow with his hands and at the same time the old man noticed from where he sat that the animal had no milk. He saw Judson get up and come walking fast towards the shack. He came and stood under the window where the old man was sitting and looked up.

'Cow's got no milk,' he said.

The old man leaned through the open window, placing both his hands on the sill.

'You lousy bastard, you've stole it.'

'I didn't take it,' said Judson. 'I bin asleep.'

'You stole it.' The old man was leaning farther out of the window, speaking quietly with one side of his mouth. 'I'll beat the hell out of you for this,' he said.

Judson said, 'Someone stole it in the night, a native, one of the Kikuyu. Or maybe she's sick.'

It seemed to the old man that he was telling the truth. 'We'll see,' he said, 'if she milks this evening; and now for Christ's sake, get out of my sight.'

By evening the cow had a full udder and the old man watched Judson draw two quarts of good thick milk from under her.

The next morning she was empty. In the evening she was full. On the third morning she was empty once more.

On the third night the old man went on watch. As soon as it began to get dark, he stationed himself at the open window with an old twelve-bore shot-gun lying on his lap, waiting for the thief who came and milked his cow in the night. At first it was pitch dark and he could not see the cow even, but soon a three-quarter moon came over the hills and it became light, almost as though it was daytime. But it was bitter cold because the Highlands are seven thousand feet up, and the old man shivered at his post and pulled his brown blanket closer around his shoulders. He could see the cow well now, just as well as in daylight, and the little acacia tree threw a deep shadow across the grass, for the moon was behind it.

All through the night the old man sat there watching the cow, and save when he got up once and hobbled back into the room to fetch another blanket, his eyes never left her. The cow stood placidly under the small tree, chewing her cud and gazing at the moon.

An hour before dawn her udder was full. The old man could see it; he had been watching it the whole time, and although he had not seen the movement of its swelling any more than one can see the movement of the hour hand of a watch, yet all the time he had been conscious of the filling as the milk came down. It was an hour before dawn. The moon was low, but the light had not gone. He could see the cow and the little tree and the greenness of the grass around the cow. Suddenly he jerked his head. He heard something. Surely that was a noise he heard. Yes, there it was again, a rustling in the grass right underneath the window where he was sitting. Quickly he pulled himself up and looked over the sill on to the ground.

Then he saw it. A large black snake, a mamba, eight feet long and as thick as a man's arm, was gliding through the wet grass, heading straight for the cow and going fast. Its small pear-shaped head was raised slightly off the ground and the movement of its body against the wetness made a clear hissing sound like gas escaping from a jet. He raised his gun to shoot. Almost at once he lowered it again, why he did not know, and he sat there not moving, watching the mamba as it approached the cow, listening to the noise it made as it went, watching it come up close to the cow and waiting for it to strike.

But it did not strike. It lifted its head and for a moment let it sway gently back and forth; then it raised the front part of its black body into the air under the udder of the cow, gently took one of the thick teats into its mouth and began to drink.

The cow did not move. There was no noise anywhere, and the body of the mamba curved gracefully up from the ground and hung under the udder of the cow. Black snake and black cow were clearly visible out there in the moonlight.

For half an hour the old man watched the mamba taking the milk of the cow. He saw the gentle pulsing of its black body as it drew the liquid out of the udder and he saw it, after a time, change from one teat to another until at last there was no longer any milk left. Then the mamba gently lowered itself to the ground and slid back through the grass in the direction whence it came. Once more it made a clear hissing noise as it went, and once more it passed underneath the window where the old man sat, leaving a thin dark trail in the wet grass where it had gone. Then it disappeared behind the shack.

Slowly the moon went down behind the ridge of Mount Kenya. Almost at the same time the sun rose up out of the escarpment in the east and Judson came out of his hut with the four-gallon kerosene tin in his hand, walking sleepily towards the cow, dragging his feet in the heavy dew as he went. The old man watched him coming and waited. Judson bent down and felt the udder with his hand and, as he did so, the old man shouted at him. Judson jumped at the sound of the old man's voice.

'It's gone again,' said the old man.

Judson said, 'Yes, cow's empty.'

'I think,' said the old man slowly, 'I think that it was a Kikuyu boy. I was dozing a bit and only woke up as he was making off. I couldn't shoot because the cow was in the way. He made off behind the cow. I'll wait for him tonight. I'll get him tonight,' he added.

Judson did not answer. He picked up his four-gallon tin and walked back to his hut.

That night the old man sat up again by the window watching the cow. For him there was this time a certain pleasure in the anticipation of what he was going to see. He knew that he would see the mamba again, but he wanted to make quite certain. And so, when the great black snake slid across the grass towards the cow an hour before sunrise, the old man leaned over the window sill and followed the movements of the mamba as it approached the cow. He saw it wait for a moment under the belly of the animal, letting its head sway slowly backwards and forwards half a dozen times before finally raising its body from the ground to take the teat of the cow into its mouth. He saw it drink the milk for half an hour, until there was none left, and he saw it lower its body and slide smoothly back behind the shack whence it came. And while he watched these things, the old man began laughing quietly with one side of his mouth.

Then the sun rose up from behind the hills, and Judson came out of his hut with the four-gallon tin in his hand, but this time he went straight to the window of the shack where the old man was sitting wrapped up in his blankets.

'What happened?' said Judson.

The old man looked down at him from his window. 'Nothing,' he said. 'Nothing happened. I dozed off again and the bastard came and took it while I was asleep. Listen, Judson,' he added, 'we got to catch this boy, otherwise you'll be going short of milk, not that that would do you any harm. But we got to catch him. I can't shoot because he's too clever; the cow's always in the way. You'll have to get him.'

'Me get him? How?'

The old man spoke very slowly. 'I think,' he said, 'I think you must hide beside the cow, right beside the cow. That is the only way you can catch him.'

Judson was rumpling his hair with his left hand.

'Today,' continued the old man, 'you will dig a shallow trench right beside the cow. If you lie in it and if I cover you over with hay and grass, the thief won't notice you until he's right alongside.'

'He may have a knife,' Judson said.

'No, he won't have a knife. You take your stick. That's all you'll need.'

Judson said, 'Yes, I'll take my stick. When he comes, I'll jump up and beat him with my stick.' Then suddenly he seemed to remember something. 'What about her chewing?' he said. 'Couldn't stand her chewing all night, crunching and crunching, crunching spit and grass like it was pebbles. Couldn't stand that all night,' and he began twisting again at his left ear with his hand.

'You'll do as you're bloody well told,' said the old man.

That day Judson dug his trench beside the cow which was to be tethered to the small acacia tree so that she could not wander about the field. Then, as evening came and as he was preparing to lie down in the trench for the night, the old man came to the door of his shack and said, 'No point in doing anything until early morning. They won't come till the cow's full. Come in here and wait; it's warmer than your filthy little hut.'

Judson had never been invited into the old man's shack before. He followed him in, happy that he would not have to lie all night in the trench. There was a candle burning in the room. It was stuck into the neck of a beer bottle and the bottle was on the table.

'Make some tea,' said the old man, pointing to the Primus stove standing on the floor. Judson lit the stove and made tea. The two of them sat down on a couple of wooden boxes and began to drink. The old man drank his hot and made loud sucking noises as he drank. Judson kept blowing on his, sipping it cautiously and watching the old man over the top of his cup. The old man went on sucking away at his tea until suddenly Judson said, 'Stop.' He said it quietly, plaintively almost, and as he said it he began to twitch around the corners of his eyes and around his mouth.

'What?' said the old man.

Judson said, 'That noise, that sucking noise you're making.'

The old man put down his cup and regarded the other quietly for a few moments, then he said, 'How many dogs you killed in your time, Judson?'

There was no answer.

'I said how many? How many dogs?'

Judson began picking the tea leaves out of his cup and sticking them on to the back of his left hand. The old man was leaning forward on his box.

'How many dogs, Judson?'

Judson began to hurry with his tea leaves. He jabbed his fingers into his empty cup, picked out a tea leaf, pressed

94

it quickly on to the back of his hand and quickly went back for another. When there were not many left and he did not find one immediately, he bent over and peered closely into the cup, trying to find the ones that remained. The back of the hand which held the cup was covered with wet black tea leaves.

'Judson!' The old man shouted, and one side of his mouth opened and shut like a pair of tongs. The candle flame flickered and became still again.

Then quietly and very slowly, coaxingly, as someone to a child. 'In all your life, how many dogs has it been?'

Judson said, 'Why should I tell you?' He did not look up. He was picking the tea leaves off the back of his hand one by one and returning them to the cup.

'I want to know, Judson.' The old man was speaking very gently. 'I'm getting keen about this too. Let's talk about it and make some plans for more fun.'

Judson looked up. A ball of saliva rolled down his chin, hung for a moment in the air, snapped and fell to the floor.

'I only kill 'em because of a noise.'

'How often've you done it? I'd love to know how often.'

'Lots of times long ago.'

'How? Tell me how you used to do it. What way did you like best?'

No answer.

'Tell me, Judson. I'd love to know.'

'I don't see why I should. It's a secret.'

'I won't tell. I swear I won't tell.'

'Well, if you'll promise.' Judson shifted his seat closer

and spoke in a whisper. 'Once I waited till one was sleeping, then I got a big stone and dropped it on his head.'

The old man got up and poured himself a cup of tea. 'You didn't kill mine like that.'

'I didn't have time. The noise was so bad, the licking, and I just had to do it quick.'

'You didn't even kill him.'

'I stopped the noise.'

The old man went over to the door and looked out. It was dark. The moon had not yet risen, but the night was clear and cold with many stars. In the east there was a little paleness in the sky, and as he watched, the paleness grew and it changed from a paleness into a brightness, spreading over the sky so that the light was reflected and held by the small drops of dew upon the grass along the Highlands; and slowly, the moon rose up over the hills. The old man turned and said, 'Better get ready. Never know; they might come early tonight.'

Judson got up and the two of them went outside. Judson lay down in the shallow trench beside the cow and the old man covered him over with grass, so that only his head peeped out above the ground. 'I shall be watching, too,' he said, 'from the window. If I give a shout, jump up and catch him.'

He hobbled back to the shack, went upstairs, wrapped himself in blankets and took up his position by the window. It was early still. The moon was nearly full and it was climbing. It shone upon the snow on the summit of Mount Kenya.

After an hour the old man shouted out of the window, 'Are you still awake, Judson?'

'Yes,' he answered, 'I'm awake.'

'Don't go to sleep,' said the old man. 'Whatever you do, don't go to sleep.'

'Cow's crunching all the time,' said Judson.

'Good, and I'll shoot you if you get up now,' said the old man.

'You'll shoot me?'

'I said, "I'll shoot you if you get up now."'

A gentle sobbing noise came up from where Judson lay, a strange gasping sound as though a child was trying not to cry, and in the middle of it, Judson's voice, 'I've got to move; please let me move. This crunching.'

'If you get up,' said the old man, 'I'll shoot you in the belly.'

For another hour or so the sobbing continued, then quite suddenly it stopped.

Just before four o'clock it began to get very cold and the old man huddled deeper into his blankets and shouted, 'Are you cold out there, Judson? Are you cold?'

'Yes,' came the answer. 'So cold. But I don't mind because cow's not crunching any more. She's asleep.'

The old man said, 'What are you going to do with the thief when you catch him?'

'I don't know.'

'Will you kill him?'

A pause.

'I don't know. I'll just go for him.'

'I'll watch,' said the old man. 'It ought to be fun.' He was leaning out of the window with his arms resting on the sill.

Then he heard the hiss under the window sill, and looked over and saw the black mamba, sliding through the grass towards the cow, going fast and holding its head just a little above the ground as it went.

When the mamba was five yards away, the old man shouted. He cupped his hands to his mouth and shouted, 'Here he comes, Judson; here he comes. Go and get him.'

Judson lifted his head quickly and looked up. As he did so he saw the mamba and the mamba saw him. There was a second, or perhaps two, when the snake stopped, drew back and raised the front part of its body in the air. Then the stroke. Just a flash of black and a slight thump as it took him in the chest. Judson screamed, a long, high-pitched scream which did not rise or fall, but held its note until gradually it faded into nothingness and there was silence. Now he was standing up, ripping open his shirt, feeling for the place in his chest, whimpering quietly, moaning and breathing hard with his mouth wide open. And all the while the old man sat quietly at the open window, leaning forward and never taking his eyes away from the one below.

Everything comes very quick when one is bitten by a black mamba, and almost at once the poison began to work. It threw him to the ground, where he lay humping his back and rolling around on the grass. He no longer made any noise. It was all very quiet, as though a man of great strength was wrestling with a giant whom one could not see, and it was as though the giant was twisting him and not letting him get up, stretching his arms through the fork of his legs and pushing his knees up under his chin.

Then he began pulling up the grass with his hands and soon after that he lay on his back kicking gently with his legs. But he didn't last very long. He gave a quick wriggle, humped his back again, turning over as he did it, then he lay on the ground quite still, lying on his stomach with his right knee drawn up underneath his chest and his hands stretched out above his head.

Still the old man sat by the window, and even after it was all over, he stayed where he was and did not stir. There was a movement in the shadow under the acacia tree and the mamba came forward slowly towards the cow. It came forward a little, stopped, raised its head, waited, lowered its head, and slid forward again right under the belly of the animal. It raised itself into the air and took one of the brown teats in its mouth and began to drink. The old man sat watching the mamba taking the milk of the cow, and once again he saw the gentle pulsing of its body as it drew the liquid out of the udder.

While the snake was still drinking, the old man got up and moved away from the window.

'You can have his share,' he said quietly. 'We don't mind you having his share,' and as he spoke he glanced back and saw again the black body of the mamba curving upwards from the ground, joining with the belly of the cow.

'Yes,' he said again, 'we don't mind your having his share.'

The Landlady

First published in the *New Yorker*,
28 November 1959

Billy Weaver had travelled down from London on the slow afternoon train, with a change at Reading on the way, and by the time he got to Bath it was about nine o'clock in the evening and the moon was coming up out of a clear starry sky over the houses opposite the station entrance. But the air was deadly cold and the wind was like a flat blade of ice on his cheeks.

'Excuse me,' he said, 'but is there a fairly cheap hotel not too far away from here?'

'Try the Bell and Dragon,' the porter answered, pointing down the road. 'They might take you in. It's about a quarter of a mile along on the other side.'

Billy thanked him and picked up his suitcase and set out to walk the quarter-mile to the Bell and Dragon. He had never been to Bath before. He didn't know anyone who lived there. But Mr Greenslade at the Head Office in London had told him it was a splendid town. 'Find your own lodgings,' he had said, 'and then go along and report to the Branch Manager as soon as you've got yourself settled.'

Billy was seventeen years old. He was wearing a new navy-blue overcoat, a new brown trilby hat, and a new brown suit, and he was feeling fine. He walked briskly down the street. He was trying to do everything briskly these days. Briskness, he had decided, was *the* one common characteristic of all successful businessmen. The big shots up at Head Office were absolutely fantastically brisk all the time. They were amazing.

There were no shops on this wide street that he was walking along, only a line of tall houses on each side, all of them identical. They had porches and pillars and four or five steps going up to their front doors, and it was obvious that once upon a time they had been very swanky residences. But now, even in the darkness, he could see that the paint was peeling from the woodwork on their doors and windows, and that the handsome white façades were cracked and blotchy from neglect.

Suddenly, in a downstairs window that was brilliantly illuminated by a street-lamp not six yards away, Billy caught sight of a printed notice propped up against the glass in one of the upper panes. It said BED AND BREAK-FAST. There was a vase of yellow chrysanthemums, tall and beautiful, standing just underneath the notice.

He stopped walking. He moved a bit closer. Green curtains (some sort of velvety material) were hanging down on either side of the window. The chrysanthemums looked wonderful beside them. He went right up and peered through the glass into the room, and the first thing he saw was a bright fire burning in the hearth. On the carpet in front of the fire, a pretty little dachshund was curled up asleep with its nose tucked into its belly. The room itself, so far as he could see in the half-darkness, was filled with pleasant furniture. There was a baby-grand piano and a big sofa and several plump armchairs; and in one corner he spotted a large parrot in a cage. Animals were usually a good sign in a place like this, Billy told himself; and all in all, it looked to him as though it would be a pretty decent house to stay in. Certainly it would be more comfortable than the Bell and Dragon.

On the other hand, a pub would be more congenial than a boarding-house. There would be beer and darts in the evenings, and lots of people to talk to, and it would probably be a good bit cheaper, too. He had stayed a couple of nights in a pub once before and he had liked it. He had never stayed in any boarding-houses, and, to be perfectly honest, he was a tiny bit frightened of them. The name itself conjured up images of watery cabbage, rapacious landladies, and a powerful smell of kippers in the living-room.

After dithering about like this in the cold for two or three minutes, Billy decided that he would walk on and take a look at the Bell and Dragon before making up his mind. He turned to go.

And now a queer thing happened to him. He was in the act of stepping back and turning away from the window when all at once his eye was caught and held in the most peculiar manner by the small notice that was there. BED AND BREAKFAST, it said. BED AND BREAKFAST, BED AND BREAKFAST, BED AND BREAKFAST. Each word was like a large black eye staring at him through the glass, holding him, compelling him, forcing him to stay where he was and not to walk away from that house, and the next thing he knew, he was actually moving across from the window to the front door of the house, climbing the steps that led up to it, and reaching for the bell.

He pressed the bell. Far away in a back room he heard it ringing, and then *at once* – it must have been at once because he hadn't even had time to take his finger from the bell-button – the door swung open and a woman was standing there.

Normally you ring the bell and you have at least a half-minute's wait before the door opens. But this dame was like a jack-in-the-box. He pressed the bell – and out she popped! It made him jump.

She was about forty-five or fifty years old, and the moment she saw him, she gave him a warm welcoming smile.

'*Please* come in,' she said pleasantly. She stepped aside, holding the door wide open, and Billy found himself automatically starting forward. The compulsion or, more accurately, the desire to follow after her into that house was extraordinarily strong.

'I saw the notice in the window,' he said, holding himself back.

'Yes, I know.'

'I was wondering about a room.'

'It's *all* ready for you, my dear,' she said. She had a round pink face and very gentle blue eyes.

'I was on my way to the Bell and Dragon,' Billy told her. 'But the notice in your window just happened to catch my eye.'

'My dear boy,' she said, 'why don't you come in out of the cold?'

'How much do you charge?'

'Five and sixpence a night, including breakfast.'

It was fantastically cheap. It was less than half of what he had been willing to pay.

'If that is too much,' she added, 'then perhaps I can reduce it just a tiny bit. Do you desire an egg for breakfast? Eggs are expensive at the moment. It would be sixpence less without the egg.'

'Five and sixpence is fine,' he answered. 'I should like very much to stay here.'

'I knew you would. Do come in.'

She seemed terribly nice. She looked exactly like the mother of one's best school-friend welcoming one into the house to stay for the Christmas holidays. Billy took off his hat, and stepped over the threshold.

'Just hang it there,' she said, 'and let me help you with your coat.'

There were no other hats or coats in the hall. There were no umbrellas, no walking-sticks – nothing.

'We have it *all* to ourselves,' she said, smiling at him over her shoulder as she led the way upstairs. 'You see, it isn't very often I have the pleasure of taking a visitor into my little nest.'

The old girl is slightly dotty, Billy told himself. But at five and sixpence a night, who gives a damn about that? 'I should've thought you'd be simply swamped with applicants,' he said politely.

'Oh, I am, my dear, I am, of course I am. But the trouble is that I'm inclined to be just a teeny weeny bit choosy and particular – if you see what I mean.'

'Ah, yes.'

'But I'm always ready. Everything is always ready day and night in this house just on the off-chance that an acceptable young gentleman will come along. And it is such a pleasure, my dear, such a very great pleasure when now and again I open the door and I see someone standing there who is just *exactly* right.' She was halfway up the stairs, and she paused with one hand on the stair-rail, turning her head and smiling down at him with pale lips. 'Like you,' she added, and her blue eyes travelled slowly all the way down the length of Billy's body, to his feet, and then up again.

On the second-floor landing she said to him, 'This floor is mine.'

They climbed up another flight. 'And this one is *all* yours,' she said. 'Here's your room. I do hope you'll like it.' She took him into a small but charming front bedroom, switching on the light as she went in.

'The morning sun comes right in the window, Mr Perkins. It *is* Mr Perkins, isn't it?'

'No,' he said. 'It's Weaver.'

'Mr Weaver. How nice. I've put a water-bottle between the sheets to air them out, Mr Weaver. It's such a comfort to have a hot water-bottle in a strange bed with clean sheets, don't you agree? And you may light the gas fire at any time if you feel chilly.'

'Thank you,' Billy said. 'Thank you ever so much.' He noticed that the bedspread had been taken off the bed, and that the bedclothes had been neatly turned back on one side, all ready for someone to get in.

'I'm so glad you appeared,' she said, looking earnestly into his face. 'I was beginning to get worried.'

'That's all right,' Billy answered brightly. 'You mustn't worry about me.' He put his suitcase on the chair and started to open it.

'And what about supper, my dear? Did you manage to get anything to eat before you came here?'

'I'm not a bit hungry, thank you,' he said. 'I think I'll just go to bed as soon as possible because tomorrow I've got to get up rather early and report to the office.'

'Very well, then. I'll leave you now so that you can unpack. But before you go to bed, would you be kind enough to pop into the sitting-room on the ground floor and sign the book? Everyone has to do that because it's the law of the land, and we don't want to go breaking any laws at *this* stage in the proceedings, do we?' She gave him a little wave of the hand and went quickly out of the room and closed the door.

Now, the fact that his landlady appeared to be slightly off her rocker didn't worry Billy in the least. After all, she not only was harmless – there was no question about that – but she was also quite obviously a kind and generous soul. He guessed that she had probably lost a son in the war, or something like that, and had never gotten over it.

So a few minutes later, after unpacking his suitcase and washing his hands, he trotted downstairs to the ground floor and entered the living-room. His landlady wasn't there, but the fire was glowing in the hearth, and the little dachshund was still sleeping soundly in front of it. The room was wonderfully warm and cosy. I'm a lucky fellow, he thought, rubbing his hands. This is a bit of all right.

He found the guest-book lying open on the piano, so he took out his pen and wrote down his name and address. There were only two other entries above his on the page, and, as one always does with guest-books, he started to read them. One was a Christopher Mulholland from Cardiff. The other was Gregory W. Temple from Bristol.

That's funny, he thought suddenly. Christopher Mulholland. It rings a bell.

Now where on earth had he heard that rather unusual name before?

Was it a boy at school? No. Was it one of his sister's numerous young men, perhaps, or a friend of his father's? No, no, it wasn't any of those. He glanced down again at the book.

Christopher Mulholland   *231 Cathedral Road, Cardiff*
Gregory W. Temple   *27 Sycamore Drive, Bristol*

As a matter of fact, now he came to think of it, he wasn't at all sure that the second name didn't have almost as much of a familiar ring about it as the first.

'Gregory Temple?' he said aloud, searching his memory. 'Christopher Mulholland? . . .'

'Such charming boys,' a voice behind him answered, and he turned and saw his landlady sailing into the room with a large silver tea-tray in her hands. She was holding it well out in front of her, and rather high up, as though the tray were a pair of reins on a frisky horse.

'They sound somehow familiar,' he said.

'They do? How interesting.'

'I'm almost positive I've heard those names before somewhere. Isn't that odd? Maybe it was in the newspapers. They weren't famous in any way, were they? I mean famous cricketers or footballers or something like that?'

'Famous,' she said, setting the tea-tray down on the low table in front of the sofa. 'Oh no, I don't think they were famous. But they were incredibly handsome, both of them, I can promise you that. They were tall and young and handsome, my dear, just exactly like you.'

Once more, Billy glanced down at the book. 'Look here,' he said, noticing the dates. 'This last entry is over two years old.'

'It is?'

'Yes, indeed. And Christopher Mulholland's is nearly a year before that – more than *three years* ago.'

'Dear me,' she said, shaking her head and heaving a dainty little sigh. 'I would never have thought it. How time does fly away from us all, doesn't it, Mr Wilkins?'

'It's Weaver,' Billy said. 'W-e-a-v-e-r.'

'Oh, of course it is!' she cried, sitting down on the sofa. 'How silly of me. I do apologize. In one ear and out the other, that's me, Mr Weaver.'

'You know something?' Billy said. 'Something that's really quite extraordinary about all this?'

'No, dear, I don't.'

'Well, you see, both of these names – Mulholland and Temple – I not only seem to remember each one of them separately, so to speak, but somehow or other, in some peculiar way, they both appear to be sort of connected together as well. As though they were both famous for the same sort of thing, if you see what I mean – like . . . well . . . like Dempsey and Tunney, for example, or Churchill and Roosevelt.'

'How amusing,' she said. 'But come over here now, dear, and sit down beside me on the sofa and I'll give you a nice cup of tea and a ginger biscuit before you go to bed.'

'You really shouldn't bother,' Billy said. 'I didn't mean you to do anything like that.' He stood by the piano, watching her as she fussed about with the cups and saucers. He noticed that she had small, white, quickly moving hands, and red fingernails.

'I'm almost positive it was in the newspapers I saw them,' Billy said. 'I'll think of it in a second. I'm sure I will.'

There is nothing more tantalizing than a thing like this that lingers just outside the borders of one's memory. He hated to give up.

'Now wait a minute,' he said. 'Wait just a minute. Mulholland . . . Christopher Mulholland . . . wasn't *that* the name of the Eton schoolboy who was on a walking-tour through the West Country, and then all of a sudden . . .'

'Milk?' she said. 'And sugar?'

'Yes, please. And then all of a sudden . . .'

'Eton schoolboy?' she said. 'Oh no, my dear, that can't possibly be right because *my* Mr Mulholland was certainly not an Eton schoolboy when he came to me. He was a Cambridge undergraduate. Come over here now and sit next to me and warm yourself in front of this lovely fire. Come on. Your tea's all ready for you.' She patted the empty place beside her on the sofa, and she sat there smiling at Billy and waiting for him to come over.

He crossed the room slowly, and sat down on the edge of the sofa. She placed his teacup on the table in front of him.

'*There* we are,' she said. 'How nice and cosy this is, isn't it?'

Billy started sipping his tea. She did the same. For half a minute or so, neither of them spoke. But Billy knew that she was looking at him. Her body was half turned towards him, and he could feel her eyes resting on his face, watching him over the rim of her teacup. Now and again, he caught a whiff of a peculiar smell that seemed to emanate directly from her person. It was not in the least unpleasant, and it reminded him – well, he wasn't quite sure what it reminded him of. Pickled walnuts? New leather? Or was it the corridors of a hospital?

At length, she said, 'Mr Mulholland was a great one for his tea. Never in my life have I seen anyone drink as much tea as dear, sweet Mr Mulholland.'

'I suppose he left fairly recently,' Billy said. He was still puzzling his head about the two names. He was positive now that he had seen them in the newspapers – in the headlines.

'Left?' she said, arching her brows. 'But my dear boy, he never left. He's still here. Mr Temple is also here. They're on the fourth floor, both of them together.'

Billy set his cup down slowly on the table and stared at his landlady. She smiled back at him, and then she put out one of her white hands and patted him comfortingly on the knee. 'How old are you, my dear?' she asked.

'Seventeen.'

'Seventeen!' she cried. 'Oh, it's the perfect age! Mr Mulholland was also seventeen. But I think he was a trifle shorter than you are; in fact I'm sure he was, and his teeth weren't *quite* so white. You have the most beautiful teeth, Mr Weaver, did you know that?'

'They're not as good as they look,' Billy said. 'They've got simply masses of fillings in them at the back.'

'Mr Temple, of course, was a little older,' she said, ignoring his remark. 'He was actually twenty-eight. And yet I never would have guessed it if he hadn't told me, never in my whole life. There wasn't a *blemish* on his body.'

'A what?' Billy said.

'His skin was *just* like a baby's.'

There was a pause. Billy picked up his teacup and took another sip of his tea, then he set it down again gently in its saucer. He waited for her to say something else, but she seemed to have lapsed into another of her silences. He sat there staring straight ahead of him into the far corner of the room, biting his lower lip.

'That parrot,' he said at last. 'You know something? It had me completely fooled when I first saw it through the window. I could have sworn it was alive.'

'Alas, no longer.'

'It's most terribly clever the way it's been done,' he said. 'It doesn't look in the least bit dead. Who did it?'

'I did.'

'*You* did?'

'Of course,' she said. 'And have you met my little Basil as well?' She nodded towards the dachshund curled up so comfortably in front of the fire. Billy looked at it. And suddenly, he realized that this animal had all the time been just as silent and motionless as the parrot. He put out a hand and touched it gently on the top of its back. The back was hard and cold, and when he pushed the hair to one side with his fingers, he could see the skin underneath, greyish-black and dry and perfectly preserved.

'Good gracious me,' he said. 'How absolutely fascinating.' He turned away from the dog and stared with deep admiration at the little woman beside him on the sofa. 'It must be most awfully difficult to do a thing like that.'

'Not in the least,' she said. 'I stuff *all* my little pets myself when they pass away. Will you have another cup of tea?'

'No, thank you,' Billy said. The tea tasted faintly of bitter almonds, and he didn't much care for it.

'You did sign the book, didn't you?'

'Oh yes.'

'That's good. Because later on, if I happen to forget what you were called, then I could always come down here and look it up. I still do that almost every day with Mr Mulholland and Mr . . . Mr . . .'

'Temple,' Billy said. 'Gregory Temple. Exuse my asking, but haven't there been *any* other guests here except them in the last two or three years?'

Holding her teacup high in one hand, inclining her head slightly to the left, she looked up at him out of the corners of her eyes and gave him another gentle little smile.

'No, my dear,' she said. 'Only you.'

Pig

First published in *Kiss, Kiss* (1960)

I

Once upon a time, in the City of New York, a beautiful baby boy was born into this world, and the joyful parents named him Lexington.

No sooner had the mother returned home from the hospital carrying Lexington in her arms than she said to her husband, 'Darling, now you must take me out to a most marvellous restaurant for dinner so that we can celebrate the arrival of our son and heir.'

Her husband embraced her tenderly and told her that any woman who could produce such a beautiful child as Lexington deserved to go absolutely any place she wanted. But was she strong enough yet, he inquired, to start running around the city late at night?

No, she said, she wasn't. But what the hell.

So that evening they both dressed themselves up in fancy clothes, and leaving little Lexington in care of a trained infant's nurse who was costing them twenty dollars a day and was Scottish into the bargain, they went out to the finest and most expensive restaurant in town. There they each ate a giant lobster and drank a bottle of champagne between them, and after that, they went on to a nightclub, where they drank another bottle of champagne and then sat holding hands for several hours while they recalled and discussed and admired each individual physical feature of their lovely newborn son.

They arrived back at their house on the East Side of Manhattan at around two o'clock in the morning and the husband paid off the taxi-driver and then began feeling in his pockets for the key to the front door. After a while, he announced that he must have left it in the pocket of his other suit, and he suggested they ring the bell and get the nurse to come down and let them in. An infant's nurse at twenty dollars a day must expect to be hauled out of bed occasionally in the night, the husband said.

So he rang the bell. They waited. Nothing happened. He rang it again, long and loud. They waited another minute. Then they both stepped back on to the street and shouted the nurse's name (McPottle) up at the nursery windows on the third floor, but there was still no response. The house was dark and silent. The wife began to grow apprehensive. Her baby was imprisoned in this place, she told herself. Alone with McPottle. And who was McPottle? They had known her for two days, that was all, and she had a thin mouth, a small disapproving eye, and a starchy bosom, and quite clearly she was in the habit of sleeping much too soundly for safety. If she couldn't hear the front-door bell, then how on earth did she expect to hear a baby crying? Why, this very second the poor thing might be swallowing its tongue or suffocating on its pillow.

'He doesn't use a pillow,' the husband said. 'You are not to worry. But I'll get you in if that's what you want.' He was feeling rather superb after all the champagne, and now he bent down and undid the laces of one of his black patent-leather shoes, and took it off. Then, holding it by the toe, he flung it hard and straight right through the dining-room window on the ground floor.

'There you are,' he said, grinning. 'We'll deduct it from McPottle's wages.'

He stepped forward and very carefully put a hand through the hole in the glass and released the catch. Then he raised the window.

'I shall lift you in first, little mother,' he said, and he took his wife round the waist and lifted her off the ground. This brought her big red mouth up level with his own, and very close, so he started kissing her. He knew from experience that women like very much to be kissed in this position, with their bodies held tight and their legs dangling in the air, so he went on doing it for quite a long time, and she wiggled her feet, and made loud gulping noises down in her throat. Finally, the husband turned her round and began easing her gently through the open window into the dining-room. At this point, a police patrol car came nosing silently along the street towards them. It stopped about thirty yards away, and three cops of Irish extraction leaped out of the car and started running in the direction of the husband and wife, brandishing revolvers.

'Stick 'em up!' the cops shouted. 'Stick 'em up!' But it was impossible for the husband to obey this order without letting go of his wife, and had he done this she would either have fallen to the ground or would have been left dangling half in and half out of the house, which is a terribly uncomfortable position for a woman; so he continued gallantly to push her upwards and inwards through the window. The cops, all of whom had received medals before for killing robbers, opened fire immediately, and although they were still running, and although the wife in particular was presenting them with a very small target indeed, they succeeded in scoring several direct hits on each body – sufficient anyway to prove fatal in both cases.

Thus, when he was no more then twelve days old, little Lexington became an orphan.

II

The news of this killing, for which the three policemen subsequently received citations, was eagerly conveyed to all relatives of the deceased couple by newspaper reporters, and the next morning, the closest of these relatives, as well as a couple of undertakers, three lawyers and a priest, climbed into taxis and set out for the house with the broken window. They assembled in the living-room, men and women both, and they sat around in a circle on the sofas and armchairs, smoking cigarettes and sipping sherry and debating what on earth should be done now with the baby upstairs, the orphan Lexington.

It soon became apparent that none of the relatives was particularly keen to assume responsibility for the child, and the discussions and arguments continued all through the day. Everybody declared an enormous, almost an irresistible desire to look after him, and would have done so with the greatest of pleasure were it not for the fact that their apartment was too small, or that they already had one baby and couldn't possibly afford another, or that they wouldn't know what to do with the poor little thing when they went abroad in the summer, or that they were getting on in years, which surely would be most unfair to the boy when he grew up, and so on and so forth. They all knew, of course, that the father had been heavily in debt for a long time and that the house was mortgaged and that consequently there would be no money at all to go with the child.

They were still arguing like mad at six in the evening when suddenly, in the middle of it all, an old aunt of the deceased father (her name was Glosspan) swept in from Virginia, and without even removing her hat and coat, not even pausing to sit down, ignoring all offers of a martini, a whisky, a sherry, she announced firmly to the assembled relatives that she herself intended to take sole charge of the infant boy from then on. What was more, she said, she would assume full financial responsibility on all counts, including education, and everyone else could go on back home where they belonged and give their consciences a rest. So saying, she trotted upstairs to the nursery and snatched Lexington from his cradle and swept out of the house with the baby clutched tightly in her arms, while the relatives simply sat and stared and smiled and looked relieved, and McPottle the nurse stood stiff with disapproval at the head of the stairs, her lips compressed, her arms folded across her starchy bosom.

And thus it was that the infant Lexington, when he was thirteen days old, left the City of New York and travelled southward to live with his Great Aunt Glosspan in the State of Virginia.

III

Aunt Glosspan was nearly seventy when she became guardian to Lexington, but to look at her you would never have guessed it for one minute. She was as sprightly as a woman half her age, with a small, wrinkled, but still quite beautiful face and two lovely brown eyes that sparkled at you in the nicest way. She was also a spinster, though you would never have guessed that either, for there was nothing spinsterish about Aunt Glosspan. She was never bitter or gloomy or irritable; she didn't have a moustache; and she wasn't in the least bit jealous of other people, which in itself is something you can seldom say about either a spinster or a virgin lady, although of course it is not known for certain whether Aunt Glosspan qualified on both counts.

But she was an eccentric old woman, there was no doubt about that. For the past thirty years she had lived a strange isolated life all by herself in a tiny cottage high up on the slopes of the Blue Ridge Mountains, several miles from the nearest village. She had five acres of pasture, a plot for growing vegetables, a flower garden, three cows, a dozen hens and a fine cockerel.

And now she had little Lexington as well.

She was a strict vegetarian and regarded the consumption of animal flesh as not only unhealthy and disgusting, but horribly cruel. She lived upon lovely clean foods like milk, butter, eggs, cheese, vegetables, nuts, herbs and fruit, and she rejoiced in the conviction that no living creature would be slaughtered on her account, not even a shrimp. Once, when a brown hen of hers passed away in the prime of life from being eggbound, Aunt Glosspan was so distressed that she nearly gave up egg-eating altogether.

She knew not the first thing about babies, but that didn't worry her in the least. At the railway station in New York, while waiting for the train that would take her and Lexington back to Virginia, she bought six feeding-bottles, two dozen diapers, a box of safety pins, a carton of milk for the journey and a small paper-covered book called *The Care of Infants*. What more could anyone want? And when the train got going, she fed the baby some milk, changing its nappies after a fashion, and laid it down on the seat to sleep. Then she read *The Care of Infants* from cover to cover.

'There is no problem here,' she said, throwing the book out the window. 'No problem at all.'

And curiously enough there wasn't. Back home in the cottage everything went just as smoothly as could be. Little Lexington drank his milk and belched and yelled and slept exactly as a good baby should, and Aunt Glosspan glowed with joy whenever she looked at him, and showered him with kisses all day long.

IV

By the time he was six years old, young Lexington had grown into a most beautiful boy with long golden hair and deep blue eyes the colour of cornflowers. He was bright and cheerful, and already he was learning to help his old aunt in all sorts of different ways around the property, collecting the eggs from the chicken house, turning the handle of the butter churn, digging up potatoes in the vegetable garden, and searching for wild herbs on the side of the mountain. Soon, Aunt Glosspan told herself, she would have to start thinking about his education.

But she couldn't bear the thought of sending him away to school. She loved him so much now that it would kill her to be parted from him for any length of time. There was, of course, that village school down in the valley, but it was a dreadful-looking place, and if she sent him there she just knew they would start forcing him to eat meat the very first day he arrived.

'You know what, my darling?' she said to him one day when he was sitting on a stool in the kitchen watching her make cheese. 'I don't really see why I shouldn't give you your lessons myself.'

The boy looked up at her with his large blue eyes, and gave her a lovely trusting smile. 'That would be nice,' he said.

'And the very first thing I should do would be to teach you how to cook.'

'I think I would like that, Aunt Glosspan.'

'Whether you like it or not, you're going to have to learn some time,' she said. 'Vegetarians like us don't have nearly so many foods to choose from as ordinary people, and therefore they must learn to be doubly expert with what they have.'

'Aunt Glosspan,' the boy said, 'what *do* ordinary people eat that we don't?'

'Animals,' she answered, tossing her head in disgust.

'You mean *live* animals?'

'No,' she said. 'Dead ones.'

The boy considered this for a moment.

'You mean when they die they *eat* them instead of *burying* them?'

'They don't wait for them to die, my pet. They kill them.'

'How do they kill them, Aunt Glosspan?'

'They usually slit their throats with a knife.'

'But what *kind* of animals?'

'Cows and pigs mostly, and sheep.'

'Cows!' the boy cried. 'You mean like Daisy and Snowdrop and Lily?'

'Exactly, my dear.'

'But *how* do they eat them, Aunt Glosspan?'

'They cut them up into bits and they cook the bits. They like it best when it's all red and bloody and sticking to the bones. They love to eat lumps of cow's flesh with the blood oozing out of it.'

'Pigs too?'

'They adore pigs.'

'Lumps of bloody pig's meat,' the boy said. 'Imagine that. What else do they eat, Aunt Glosspan?'

'Chickens.'

'Chickens!'

'Millions of them.'

'Feathers and all?'

'No, dear, not the feathers. Now run along outside and get Aunt Glosspan a bunch of chives, will you, my darling?'

Shortly after that, the lessons began. They covered five subjects, reading, writing, geography, arithmetic and cooking, but the latter was by far the most popular with both teacher and pupil. In fact, it very soon became apparent that young Lexington possessed a truly remarkable talent in this direction. He was a born cook. He was dextrous and quick. He could handle his pans like a juggler. He could slice a single potato into twenty paper-thin slivers in less time than it took his aunt to peel it. His palate was exquisitely sensitive, and he could taste a pot of strong onion soup and immediately detect the presence of a single tiny leaf of sage. In so young a boy, all this was a bit bewildering to Aunt Glosspan, and to tell the truth she didn't quite know what to make of it. But she was proud as proud could be, all the same, and predicted a brilliant future for the child.

'What a mercy it is,' she said, 'that I have such a wonderful little fellow to look after me in my dotage.' And a couple of years later, she retired from the kitchen for good, leaving Lexington in sole charge of all household cooking. The boy was now ten years old, and Aunt Glosspan was nearly eighty.

V

With the kitchen to himself, Lexington straight away began experimenting with dishes of his own invention. The old favourites no longer interested him. He had a violent urge to create. There were hundreds of fresh ideas in his head. 'I will begin,' he said, 'by devising a chestnut soufflé.' He made it and served it up for supper that very night. It was terrific. 'You are a genius!' Aunt Glosspan cried, leaping up from her chair and kissing him on both cheeks. 'You will make history!'

From then on, hardly a day went by without some new delectable creation being set upon the table. There was Brazil-nut soup, hominy cutlets, vegetable ragout, dandelion omelette, cream-cheese fritters, stuffed-cabbage surprise, stewed foggage, shallots *à la bonne femme*, beetroot mousse piquant, prunes Stroganoff, Dutch rarebit, turnips on horseback, flaming spruce-needle tarts, and many many other beautiful compositions. Never before in her life, Aunt Glosspan declared, had she tasted such food as this; and in the mornings, long before lunch was due, she would go out on to the porch and sit there in her rocking-chair, speculating about the coming meal, licking her chops, sniffing the aromas that came wafting out through the kitchen window.

'What's that you're making in there today, boy?' she would call out.

'Try to guess, Aunt Glosspan.'

'Smells like a bit of salsify fritters to me,' she would say, sniffing vigorously.

Then out he would come, this ten-year-old child, a little grin of triumph on his face, and in his hands a big steaming pot of the most heavenly stew made entirely of parsnips and lovage.

'You know what you ought to do,' his aunt said to

him, gobbling the stew. 'You ought to set yourself down this very minute with paper and pencil and write a cooking-book.'

He looked at her across the table, chewing his parsnips slowly.

'Why not?' she cried. 'I've taught you how to write and I've taught you how to cook and now all you've got to do is put the two things together. You write a cooking-book, my darling, and it'll make you famous the whole world over.'

'All right,' he said. 'I will.'

And that very day, Lexington began writing the first page of that monumental work which was to occupy him for the rest of his life. He called it *Eat Good and Healthy*.

VI

Seven years later, by the time he was seventeen, he had recorded over nine thousand different recipes, all of them original, all of them delicious.

But now, suddenly, his labours were interrupted by the tragic death of Aunt Glosspan. She was afflicted in the night by a violent seizure, and Lexington, who had rushed into her bedroom to see what all the noise was about, found her lying on her bed yelling and cussing and twisting herself up into all manner of complicated knots. Indeed, she was a terrible sight to behold, and the agitated youth danced round her in his pyjamas, wringing his hands, and wondering what on earth he should do. Finally, in an effort to cool her down, he fetched a bucket of water from the pond in the cow field and tipped it over her head, but this only intensified the paroxysms, and the old lady expired within the hour.

'This is really too bad,' the poor boy said, pinching her several times to make sure that she was dead. 'And how sudden! How quick and sudden! Why only a few hours ago she seemed in the very best of spirits. She even took three large helpings of my most recent creation, devilled mushroom-burgers, and told me how succulent it was.'

After weeping bitterly for several minutes, for he had loved his aunt very much, he pulled himself together and carried her outside and buried her behind the cowshed.

The next day, while tidying up her belongings, he came across an envelope that was addressed to him in Aunt Glosspan's handwriting. He opened it and drew out two fifty-dollar bills and a letter. 'Darling boy,' the letter said.

I know that you have never yet been down the mountain since you were thirteen days old, but as soon as I die you must put on a pair of shoes and a clean shirt and walk down to the village and find the doctor. Ask the doctor to give you a death certificate to prove that I am dead. Then take this certificate to my lawyer, a man called Mr Samuel Zuckermann, who lives in New York City and who has a copy of my will. Mr Zuckermann will arrange everything. The cash in this envelope is to pay the doctor for the certificate and to cover the cost of your journey to New York. Mr Zuckermann will give you more money when you get there, and it is my earnest wish that you use it to further your researches into culinary and vegetarian matters, and that you continue to work upon that great book of yours until you are satisfied that it is complete in every way. Your loving aunt – Glosspan.

Lexington, who had always done everything his aunt told him, pocketed the money, put on a pair of shoes and a clean shirt, and went down the mountain to the village where the doctor lived.

'Old Glosspan?' the doctor said. 'My God, is *she* dead?'

'Certainly she's dead,' the youth answered. 'If you will come back home with me now I'll dig her up and you can see for yourself.'

'How deep did you bury her?' the doctor asked.

'Six or seven feet down, I should think.'

'And how long ago?'

'Oh, about eight hours.'

'Then she's dead,' the doctor announced. 'Here's the certificate.'

VII

Our hero now set out for the City of New York to find Mr Samuel Zuckermann. He travelled on foot, and he slept under hedges, and he lived on berries and wild herbs, and it took him sixteen days to reach the metropolis.

'What a fabulous place this is!' he cried as he stood at the corner of Fifty-seventh Street and Fifth Avenue, staring around him. 'There are no cows or chickens anywhere, and none of the women looks in the least like Aunt Glosspan.'

As for Mr Samuel Zuckermann, he looked like nothing that Lexington had ever seen before.

He was a small spongy man with livid jowls and a huge magenta nose, and when he smiled, bits of gold flashed at you marvellously from lots of different places inside his mouth. In his luxurious office, he shook Lexington warmly by the hand and congratulated him upon his aunt's death.

'I suppose you knew that your dearly beloved guardian was a woman of considerable wealth?' he said.

'You mean the cows and the chickens?'

'I mean half a million bucks,' Mr Zuckermann said.

'How much?'

'Half a million dollars, my boy. And she's left it all to you.' Mr Zuckermann leaned back in his chair and clasped his hands over his spongy paunch. At the same time, he began secretly working his right forefinger in through his waistcoat and under his shirt so as to scratch the skin around the circumference of his navel – a favourite exercise of his, and one that gave him a peculiar pleasure. 'Of course, I shall have to deduct fifty per cent for my services,' he said, 'but that still leaves you with two hundred and fifty grand.'

'I am rich!' Lexington cried. 'This is wonderful! How soon can I have the money?'

'Well,' Mr Zuckermann said, 'luckily for you, I happen to be on rather cordial terms with the tax authorities around here, and I am confident that I shall be able to persuade them to waive all death duties and back taxes.'

'How kind you are,' murmured Lexington.

'I shall naturally have to give somebody a small honorarium.'

'Whatever you say, Mr Zuckermann.'

'I think a hundred thousand would be sufficient.'

'Good gracious, isn't that rather excessive?'

'Never undertip a tax-inspector or a policeman,' Mr Zuckermann said. 'Remember that.'

'But how much does it leave for me?' the youth asked meekly.

'One hundred and fifty thousand. But then you've got the funeral expenses to pay out of that.'

'*Funeral* expenses?'

'You've got to pay the funeral parlour. Surely you know that?'

'But I buried her myself, Mr Zuckermann, behind the cowshed.'

'I don't doubt it,' the lawyer said. 'So what?'

'I never used a funeral parlour.'

'Listen,' Mr Zuckermann said patiently. 'You may not know it, but there is a law in this State which says that no beneficiary under a will may receive a single penny of his inheritance until the funeral parlour has been paid in full.'

'You mean that's a *law*?'

'Certainly it's a law, and a very good one it is, too. The funeral parlour is one of our great national institutions. It must be protected at all cost.'

Mr Zuckermann himself, together with a group of public-spirited doctors, controlled a corporation that owned a chain of nine lavish funeral parlours in the city, not to mention a casket factory in Brooklyn and a post-graduate school for embalmers in Washington Heights. The celebration of death was therefore a deeply religious affair in Mr Zuckermann's eyes. In fact, the whole business affected him profoundly, almost as profoundly, one might say, as the birth of Christ affected the shopkeeper.

'You had no right to go out and bury your aunt like that,' he said. 'None at all.'

'I'm very sorry, Mr Zuckermann.'

'Why, it's downright subversive.'

'I'll do whatever you say, Mr Zuckermann. All I want to know is how much I'm going to get in the end, when everything's paid.'

There was a pause. Mr Zuckermann sighed and frowned and continued secretly to run the tip of his finger round the rim of his navel.

'Shall we say fifteen thousand?' he suggested, flashing a big gold smile. 'That's a nice round figure.'

'Can I take it with me this afternoon?'

'I don't see why not.'

So Mr Zuckermann summoned his chief cashier and told him to give Lexington fifteen thousand dollars out of the petty cash, and to obtain a receipt. The youth, who by this time was delighted to be getting anything at all, accepted the money gratefully and stowed it away in his knapsack. Then he shook Mr Zuckermann warmly by the hand, thanked him for all his help, and went out of the office.

'The whole world is before me!' our hero cried as he emerged into the street. 'I now have fifteen thousand dollars to see me through until my book is published. And after that, of course, I shall have a great deal more.' He stood on the pavement, wondering which way to go. He turned left and began strolling slowly down the street, staring at the sights of the city.

'What a revolting smell,' he said, sniffing the air. 'I can't stand this.' His delicate olfactory nerves, tuned to receive only the most delicious kitchen aromas, were being tortured by the stench of the diesel-oil fumes pouring out of the backs of the buses.

'I must get out of this place before my nose is ruined altogether,' he said. 'But first, I've simply got to have something to eat. I'm starving.' The poor boy had had nothing but berries and wild herbs for the past two weeks, and now his stomach was yearning for solid food. I'd like a nice hominy cutlet, he told himself. Or maybe a few juicy salsify fritters.

He crossed the street and entered a small restaurant. The place was hot inside, and dark and silent. There was a strong smell of cooking-fat and cabbage water. The only other customer was a man with a brown hat on his head, crouching intently over his food, who did not look up as Lexington came in.

Our hero seated himself at a corner table and hung his knapsack on the back of his chair. This, he told himself, is going to be most interesting. In all my seventeen years I have tasted only the cooking of two people, Aunt Glosspan and myself – unless one counts Nurse McPottle, who must have heated my bottle a few times when I was an infant. But I am now about to sample the art of a new chef altogether, and perhaps, if I am lucky, I may pick up a couple of useful ideas for my book.

A waiter approached out of the shadows at the back, and stood beside the table.

'How do you do,' Lexington said. 'I should like a large hominy cutlet please. Do it twenty-five seconds each side, in a very hot skillet with sour cream, and sprinkle a pinch of lovage on it before serving – unless of course your chef knows of a more original method, in which case I should be delighted to try it.'

The waiter laid his head over to one side and looked carefully at his customer. 'You want the roast pork and cabbage?' he asked. 'That's all we got left.'

'Roast what and cabbage?'

The waiter took a soiled handkerchief from his trouser pocket and shook it open with a violent flourish, as though he were cracking a whip. Then he blew his nose loud and wet.

'You want it or don't you?' he said, wiping his nostrils.

'I haven't the foggiest idea what it is,' Lexington replied, 'but I should love to try it. You see, I am writing a cooking-book and . . .'

'One pork and cabbage!' the waiter shouted, and somewhere in the back of the restaurant, far away in the darkness, a voice answered him.

The waiter disappeared. Lexington reached into his knapsack for his personal knife and fork. These were a present from Aunt Glosspan, given him when he was six years old, made of solid silver, and he had never eaten with any other instruments since. While waiting for the food to arrive, he polished them lovingly with a piece of soft muslin.

Soon the waiter returned carrying a plate on which there lay a thick greyish-white slab of something hot. Lexington leaned forward anxiously to smell it as it was put down before him. His nostrils were wide open now to receive the scent, quivering and sniffing.

'But this is absolute heaven!' he exclaimed. 'What an aroma! It's tremendous!'

The waiter stepped back a pace, watching his customer carefully.

'Never in my life have I smelled anything as rich and wonderful as this!' our hero cried, seizing his knife and fork. 'What on earth is it made of?'

The man in the brown hat looked around and stared, then returned to his eating. The waiter was backing away towards the kitchen.

Lexington cut off a small piece of the meat, impaled it on his silver fork, and carried it up to his nose so as to smell it again. Then he popped it into his mouth and began to chew it slowly, his eyes half closed, his body tense.

'This is fantastic!' he cried. 'It is a brand-new flavour! Oh, Glosspan, my beloved Aunt, how I wish you were with me now so you could taste this remarkable dish! Waiter! Come here at once! I want you!'

The astonished waiter was now watching from the other end of the room, and he seemed reluctant to move any closer.

'If you will come and talk to me I will give you a present,'

Lexington said, waving a hundred-dollar bill. 'Please come over here and talk to me.'

The waiter sidled cautiously back to the table, snatched away the money, and held it up close to his face, peering at it from all angles. Then he slipped it quickly into his pocket.

'What can I do for you, my friend?' he asked.

'Look,' Lexington said. 'If you will tell me what this delicious dish is made of, and exactly how it is prepared, I will give you another hundred.'

'I already told you,' the man said. 'It's pork.'

'And what exactly is pork?'

'You never had roast pork before?' the waiter asked, staring.

'For heaven's sake, man, tell me what it is and stop keeping me in suspense like this.'

'It's pig,' the waiter said. 'You just bung it in the oven.'

'*Pig!*'

'All pork is pig. Didn't you know that?'

'You mean *this* is *pig's meat?*'

'I guarantee it.'

'But . . . but . . . that's impossible,' the youth stammered. 'Aunt Glosspan, who knew more about food than anyone else in the world, said that meat of any kind was disgusting, revolting, horrible, foul, nauseating and beastly. And yet this piece that I have here on my plate is without a doubt the most delicious thing that I have ever tasted. Now how on earth do you explain that? Aunt Glosspan certainly wouldn't have told me it was revolting if it wasn't.'

'Maybe your aunt didn't know how to cook it,' the waiter said.

'Is that possible?'

'You're damn right it is. Especially with pork. Pork has to be very well done or you can't eat it.'

'Eureka!' Lexington cried. 'I'll bet that's exactly what happened! She did it wrong!' He handed the man another hundred-dollar bill. 'Lead me to the kitchen,' he said. 'Introduce me to the genius who prepared this meat.'

Lexington was at once taken into the kitchen, and there he met the cook who was an elderly man with a rash on one side of his neck.

'This will cost you another hundred,' the waiter said.

Lexington was only too glad to oblige, but this time he gave the money to the cook. 'Now listen to me,' he said, 'I have to admit that I am really rather confused by what the waiter has just been telling me. Are you quite positive that the delectable dish which I have just been eating was prepared from pig's flesh?'

The cook raised his right hand and began scratching the rash on his neck.

'Well,' he said, looking at the waiter and giving him a sly wink, 'all I can tell you is that I *think* it was pig's meat.'

'You mean you're not sure?'

'One can't ever be sure.'

'Then what else could it have been?'

'Well,' the cook said, speaking very slowly and still staring at the waiter. 'There's just a chance, you see, that it might have been a piece of human stuff.'

'You mean a man?'

'Yes.'

'Good heavens.'

'Or a woman. It could have been either. They both taste the same.'

'Well – now you really do surprise me,' the youth declared.

'One lives and learns.'

'Indeed one does.'

'As a matter of fact, we've been getting an awful lot of it just lately from the butcher's in place of pork,' the cook declared.

'Have you really?'

'The trouble is, it's almost impossible to tell which is which. They're both very good.'

'The piece I had just now was simply superb.'

'I'm glad you liked it,' the cook said. 'But to be quite honest, I think that was a bit of pig. In fact, I'm almost sure it was.'

'You are?'

'Yes, I am.'

'In that case, we shall have to assume that you are right,' Lexington said. 'So now will you please tell me – and here is another hundred dollars for your trouble – will you please tell me precisely how you prepared it?'

The cook, after pocketing the money, launched out upon a colourful description of how to roast a loin of pork, while the youth, not wanting to miss a single word of so great a recipe, sat down at the kitchen table and recorded every detail in his notebook.

'Is that all?' he asked when the cook had finished.

'That's all.'

'But there must be more to it than that, surely?'

'You got to get a good piece of meat to start off with,' the cook said. 'That's half the battle. It's got to be a good hog and it's got to be butchered right, otherwise it'll turn out lousy whichever way you cook it.'

'Show me how,' Lexington said. 'Butcher me one now so I can learn.'

'We don't butcher pigs in the kitchen,' the cook said. 'That lot you just ate came from a packing-house over in the Bronx.'

'Then give me the address!'

The cook gave him the address, and our hero, after thanking them both many times for all their kindnesses, rushed outside and leaped into a taxi and headed for the Bronx.

VIII

The packing-house was a big four-storey brick building, and the air around it smelled sweet and heavy, like musk. At the main entrance gates, there was a large notice which said VISITORS WELCOME AT ANY TIME, and thus encouraged, Lexington walked through the gates and entered a cobbled yard which surrounded the building itself. He then followed a series of signposts (THIS WAY FOR THE GUIDED TOURS), and came eventually to a small corrugated-iron shed set well apart from the main building (VISITORS WAITING-ROOM). After knocking politely on the door, he went in.

There were six other people ahead of him in the waiting-room. There was a fat mother with her two little boys aged about nine and eleven. There was a bright-eyed young couple who looked as though they might be on their honeymoon. And there was a pale woman with long white gloves, who sat very upright, looking straight ahead with her hands folded on her lap. Nobody spoke. Lexington wondered whether they were all writing cooking-books, like himself, but when he put this question to them aloud, he got no answer. The grown-ups merely smiled mysteriously to themselves and shook their heads, and the two children stared at him as though they were seeing a lunatic.

Soon, the door opened and a man with a merry pink face popped his head into the room and said, 'Next, please.' The mother and the two boys got up and went out.

About ten minutes later, the same man returned. 'Next, please,' he said again, and the honeymoon couple jumped up and followed him outside.

Two new visitors came in and sat down – a middle-aged husband and a middle-aged wife, the wife carrying a wicker shopping-basket containing groceries.

'Next, please,' said the guide, and the woman with the long white gloves got up and left.

Several more people came in and took their places on the stiff-backed wooden chairs.

Soon the guide returned for the third time, and now it was Lexington's turn to go outside.

'Follow me, please,' the guide said, leading the youth across the yard towards the main building.

'How exciting this is!' Lexington cried, hopping from one foot to the other. 'I only wish that my dear Aunt Glosspan could be with me now to see what I am going to see.'

'I myself only do the preliminaries,' the guide said. 'Then I shall hand you over to someone else.'

'Anything you say,' cried the ecstatic youth.

First they visited a large penned-in area at the back of the building where several hundred pigs were wandering around. 'Here's where they start,' the guide said. 'And over there's where they go in.'

'Where?'

'Right there.' The guide pointed to a long wooden shed that stood against the outside wall of the factory. 'We call it the shackling-pen. This way, please.'

Three men wearing long rubber boots were driving a dozen pigs into the shackling-pen just as Lexington and the guide approached, so they all went in together.

'Now,' the guide said, 'watch how they shackle them.'

Inside, the shed was simply a bare wooden room with no roof, but there was a steel cable with hooks on it that kept moving slowly along the length of one wall, parallel with the ground, about three feet up. When it reached the end of the shed, this cable suddenly changed direction and climbed vertically upwards through the open roof towards the top floor of the main building.

The twelve pigs were huddled together at the far end of the pen, standing quietly, looking apprehensive. One of the men in rubber boots pulled a length of metal chain down from the wall and advanced upon the nearest animal, approaching it from the rear. Then he bent down and quickly looped one end of the chain around one of the animal's hind legs. The other end he attached to a hook on the moving cable as it went by. The cable kept moving. The chain tightened. The pig's leg was pulled up and back, and then the pig itself began to be dragged backwards. But it didn't fall down. It was rather a nimble pig, and somehow it managed to keep its balance on three legs, hopping from foot to foot and struggling against the pull of the chain, but going back and back all the time until at the end of the pen where the cable changed direction and went vertically upwards, the creature was suddenly jerked off its feet and borne aloft. Shrill protests filled the air.

'Truly a fascinating process,' Lexington said. 'But what was that funny cracking noise it made as it went up?'

'Probably the leg,' the guide answered. 'Either that or the pelvis.'

'But doesn't that matter?'

'Why should it matter?' the guide asked. 'You don't eat the bones.'

The rubber-booted men were busy shackling the rest of the pigs, and one after another they were hooked to the moving cable and hoisted up through the roof, protesting loudly as they went.

'There's a good deal more to this recipe than just picking herbs,' Lexington said. 'Aunt Glosspan would never have made it.'

At this point, while Lexington was gazing skyward at the last pig to go up, a man in rubber boots approached him quietly from behind and looped one end of a chain round the youth's own left ankle, hooking the other end to the moving belt. The next moment, before he had time to realize what was happening, our hero was jerked off his feet and dragged backwards along the concrete floor of the shackling-pen.

'Stop!' he cried. 'Hold everything! My leg is caught!'

But nobody seemed to hear him, and five seconds later, the unhappy young man was jerked off the floor and hoisted vertically upwards through the open roof of the pen, dangling upside down by one ankle, and wriggling like a fish.

'Help!' he shouted. 'Help! There's been a frightful mistake! Stop the engines! Let me down!'

The guide removed a cigar from his mouth and looked up serenely at the rapidly ascending youth, but he said nothing. The men in rubber boots were already on their way out to collect the next batch of pigs.

'Oh save me!' our hero cried. 'Let me down! Please let me down!' But he was now approaching the top floor of the building where the moving belt curled over like a snake and entered a large hole in the wall, a kind of doorway without a door; and there, on the threshold, waiting to greet him, clothed in a dark-stained yellow rubber apron, and looking for all the world like Saint Peter at the Gates of Heaven, the sticker stood.

Lexington saw him only from upside down, and very briefly at that, but even so he noticed at once the expression of absolute peace and benevolence on the man's face, the cheerful twinkle in the eyes, the little wistful smile, and the dimples in his cheeks — and all this gave him hope.

'Hi there,' the sticker said, smiling.

'Quick! Save me!' our hero cried.

'With pleasure,' the sticker said, and taking Lexington gently by one ear with his left hand, he raised his right hand and deftly slit open the boy's jugular vein with a knife.

The belt moved on. Lexington went with it. Everything was still upside down and the blood was pouring out of his throat and getting into his eyes, but he could still see after a fashion, and he had a blurred impression of being in an enormously long room, and at the far end of the room there was a great smoking cauldron of water, and there were dark figures, half hidden in the steam, dancing round the edge of it, brandishing long poles. The conveyor-belt seemed to be travelling right over the top of the cauldron, and the pigs seemed to be dropping down one by one into the boiling water, and one of the pigs seemed to be wearing long white gloves on its front feet.

Suddenly our hero started to feel very sleepy, but it wasn't until his good strong heart had pumped the last drop of blood from his body that he passed on out of this, the best of all possible worlds, into the next.

The Boy Who Talked with Animals

First published in *The Wonderful Story of
Henry Sugar* (1977)

Not so long ago, I decided to spend a few days in the West
Indies. I was to go there for a short holiday. Friends had
told me it was marvellous. I would laze around all day,
they said, sunning myself on the silver beaches and swimming in the warm green sea.

I chose Jamaica, and flew direct from London to Kingston. The drive from Kingston airport to my hotel on the
north shore took two hours. The island was full of mountains and the mountains were covered all over with dark
tangled forests. The big Jamaican who drove the taxi told
me that up in those forests lived whole communities of
diabolical people who still practised voodoo and witch-
doctory and other magic rites. 'Don't ever go up into
those mountain forests,' he said, rolling his eyes. 'There's
things happening up there that'd make your hair turn
white in a minute!'

'What sort of things?' I asked him.

'It's better you don't ask,' he said. 'It don't pay even to
talk about it.' And that was all he would say on the
subject.

My hotel lay upon the edge of a pearly beach, and the
setting was even more beautiful than I had imagined. But
the moment I walked in through those big open front

doors, I began to feel uneasy. There was no reason for this. I couldn't see anything wrong. But the feeling was there and I couldn't shake it off. There was something weird and sinister about the place. Despite all the loveliness and the luxury, there was a whiff of danger that hung and drifted in the air like poisonous gas.

And I wasn't sure it was just the hotel. The whole island, the mountains and the forests, the black rocks along the coastline and the trees cascading with brilliant scarlet flowers, all these and many other things made me feel uncomfortable in my skin. There was something malignant crouching underneath the surface of this island. I could sense it in my bones.

My room in the hotel had a little balcony, and from there I could step straight down on to the beach. There were tall coconut palms growing all around, and every so often an enormous green nut the size of a football would fall out of the sky and drop with a thud on the sand. It was considered foolish to linger underneath a coconut palm because if one of those things landed on your head, it would smash your skull.

The Jamaican girl who came in to tidy my room told me that a wealthy American called Mr Wasserman had met his end in precisely this manner only two months before.

'You're joking,' I said to her.

'Not joking!' she cried. 'No *suh*! I sees it happening with my very own eyes!'

'But wasn't there a terrific fuss about it?' I asked.

'They hush it up,' she answered darkly. 'The hotel folks

hush it up and so do the newspaper folks because things like that are very bad for the tourist business.'

'And you say you actually saw it happen?'

'I actually saw it happen,' she said. 'Mr Wasserman, he's standing right under that very tree over there on the beach. He's got his camera out and he's pointing it at the sunset. It's a red sunset that evening, and very pretty. Then all at once, down comes a big green nut right smack on to the top of his bald head. *Wham!* And that,' she added with a touch of relish, 'is the very last sunset Mr Wasserman ever did see.'

'You mean it killed him instantly?'

'I don't know about *instantly*,' she said. 'I remember the next thing that happens is the camera falls out of his hands on to the sand. Then his arms drop down to his sides and hang there. Then he starts swaying. He sways backwards and forwards several times ever so gentle, and I'm standing there watching him, and I says to myself the poor man's gone all dizzy and maybe he's going to faint any moment. Then very very slowly he keels right over and down he goes.'

'Was he dead?'

'Dead as a doornail,' she said.

'Good heavens.'

'That's right,' she said. 'It never pays to be standing under a coconut palm when there's a breeze blowing.'

'Thank you,' I said. 'I'll remember that.'

On the evening of my second day, I was sitting on my little balcony with a book on my lap and a tall glass of rum punch in my hand. I wasn't reading the book. I was watching a small green lizard stalking another small green lizard on the balcony floor about six feet away. The stalking lizard was coming up on the other one from behind, moving forwards very slowly and very cautiously, and when he came within reach, he flicked out a long tongue and touched the other one's tail. The other one jumped round, and the two of them faced each other, motionless, glued to the floor, crouching, staring and very tense. Then suddenly, they started doing a funny little hopping dance together. They hopped up in the air. They hopped backwards. They hopped forwards. They hopped sideways. They circled one another like two boxers, hopping and prancing and dancing all the time. It was a queer thing to watch, and I guessed it was some sort of a courtship ritual they were going through. I kept very still, waiting to see what was going to happen next.

But I never saw what happened next because at that moment I became aware of a great commotion on the beach below. I glanced over and saw a crowd of people clustering around something at the water's edge. There was a narrow canoe-type fisherman's boat pulled up on the sand nearby, and all I could think of was that the fisherman had come in with a lot of fish and that the crowd was looking at it.

A haul of fish is something that has always fascinated me. I put my book aside and stood up. More people were trooping down from the hotel veranda and hurrying over the beach to join the crowd on the edge of the water. The men were wearing those frightful Bermuda shorts that came down to the knees, and their shirts were bilious with pinks and oranges and every other clashing colour you could think of. The women had better taste, and were dressed for the most part in pretty cotton dresses. Nearly everyone carried a drink in one hand.

I picked up my own drink and stepped down from the balcony on to the beach. I made a little detour around the coconut palm under which Mr Wasserman had supposedly met his end, and strode across the beautiful silvery sand to join the crowd.

But it wasn't a haul of fish they were staring at. It was a turtle, an upside-down turtle lying on its back in the sand. But what a turtle it was! It was a giant, a mammoth. I had not thought it possible for a turtle to be as enormous as this. How can I describe its size? Had it been the right way up, I think a tall man could have sat on its back without his feet touching the ground. It was perhaps five feet long and four feet across, with a high domed shell of great beauty.

The fisherman who had caught it had tipped it on to its back to stop it from getting away. There was also a thick rope tied around the middle of its shell, and one proud fisherman, slim and black and naked except for a small loincloth, stood a short way off holding the end of the rope with both hands.

Upside down it lay, this magnificent creature, with its four thick flippers waving frantically in the air, and its long wrinkled neck stretching far out of its shell. The flippers had large sharp claws on them.

'Stand back, ladies and gentlemen, please!' cried the

fisherman. 'Stand well back! Them claws is *dangerous*, man! They'll rip your arm clear away from your body!'

The crowd of hotel guests was thrilled and delighted by this spectacle. A dozen cameras were out and clicking away. Many of the women were squealing with pleasure clutching on to the arms of their men, and the men were demonstrating their lack of fear and their masculinity by making foolish remarks in loud voices.

'Make yourself a nice pair of horn-rimmed spectacles out of that shell, hey Al?'

'Darn thing must weigh over a ton!'

'You mean to say it can actually float?'

'Sure it floats. Powerful swimmer, too. Pull a boat easy.'

'He's a snapper, is he?'

'That's no snapper. Snapper turtles don't grow as big as that. But I'll tell you what. He'll snap your hand off quick enough if you get too close to him.'

'Is that true?' one of the women asked the fisherman. 'Would he snap off a person's hand?'

'He would right now,' the fisherman said, smiling with brilliant white teeth. 'He won't ever hurt you when he's in the ocean, but you catch him and pull him ashore and tip him up like this, then man alive, you'd better watch out! He'll snap at anything that comes in reach!'

'I guess I'd get a bit snappish myself,' the woman said, 'if I was in his situation.'

One idiotic man had found a plank of driftwood on the sand, and he was carrying it towards the turtle. It was a fair-sized plank, about five feet long and maybe an inch thick. He started poking one end of it at the turtle's head.

'I wouldn't do that,' the fisherman said. 'You'll only make him madder than ever.'

When the end of the plank touched the turtle's neck, the great head whipped round and the mouth opened wide and *snap*, it took the plank in its mouth and bit through it as if it were made of cheese.

'Wow!' they shouted. 'Did you see that! I'm glad it wasn't my arm!'

'Leave him alone,' the fisherman said. 'It don't help to get him all stirred up.'

A paunchy man with wide hips and very short legs came up to the fisherman and said, 'Listen, feller. I want that shell. I'll buy it from you.' And to his plump wife, he said, 'You know what I'm going to do, Mildred? I'm going to take that shell home and have it polished up by an expert. Then I'm going to place it smack in the centre of our living-room! Won't that be something?'

'Fantastic,' the plump wife said. 'Go ahead and buy it, baby.'

'Don't worry,' he said. 'It's mine already.' And to the fisherman, he said, 'How much for the shell?'

'I already sold him,' the fisherman said. 'I sold him shell and all.'

'Not so fast, feller,' the paunchy man said. 'I'll bid you higher. Come on. What'd he offer you?'

'No can do,' the fisherman said. 'I already sold him.'

'Who to?' the paunchy man said.

'To the manager.'

'What manager?'

'The manager of the hotel.'

'Did you hear that?' shouted another man. 'He's sold it to the manager of our hotel! And you know what that means? It means turtle soup, that's what it means!'

'Right you are! And turtle steak! You ever have a turtle steak, Bill?'

'I never have, Jack. But I can't wait.'

'A turtle steak's better than a beefsteak if you cook it right. It's more tender and it's got one heck of a flavour.'

'Listen,' the paunchy man said to the fisherman. 'I'm not trying to buy the meat. The manager can have the meat. He can have everything that's inside including the teeth and toenails. All I want is the shell.'

'And if I know you, baby,' his wife said, beaming at him, 'you're going to get the shell.'

I stood there listening to the conversation of these human beings. They were discussing the destruction, the consumption and the flavour of a creature who seemed, even when upside down, to be extraordinarily dignified. One thing was certain. He was senior to any of them in age. For probably one hundred and fifty years he had been cruising in the green waters of the West Indies. He was there when George Washington was President of the United States and Napoleon was being clobbered at Waterloo. He would have been a small turtle then, but he was most certainly there.

And now he was here, upside down on the beach, waiting to be sacrificed for soup and steak. He was clearly alarmed by all the noise and the shouting around him. His old wrinkled neck was straining out of its shell, and the great head was twisting this way and that as though searching for someone who would explain the reason for all this ill-treatment.

'How are you going to get him up to the hotel?' the paunchy man asked.

'Drag him up the beach with the rope,' the fisherman answered. 'The staff'll be coming along soon to take him. It's going to need ten men, all pulling at once.'

'Hey, listen!' cried a muscular young man. 'Why don't we drag him up?' The muscular young man was wearing magenta and pea-green Bermuda shorts and no shirt. He had an exceptionally hairy chest, and the absence of a shirt was obviously a calculated touch. 'What say we do a little work for our supper?' he cried, rippling his muscles. 'Come on, fellers! Who's for some exercise?'

'Great idea!' they shouted. 'Splendid scheme!'

The men handed their drinks to the women and rushed to catch hold of the rope. They ranged themselves along it as though for a tug of war, and the hairy-chested man appointed himself anchor-man and captain of the team.

'Come on, now, fellers!' he shouted. 'When I say *heave*, then all heave at once, you understand?'

The fisherman didn't like this much. 'It's better you leave this job for the hotel,' he said.

'Rubbish!' shouted hairy-chest. '*Heave*, boys, *heave*!'

They all heaved. The gigantic turtle wobbled on its back and nearly toppled over.

'Don't tip him!' yelled the fisherman. 'You're going to

tip him over if you do that! And if once he gets back on to his legs again, he'll escape for sure!'

'Cool it, laddie,' said hairy-chest in a patronizing voice. 'How can he escape? We've got a rope round him, haven't we?'

'The old turtle will drag the whole lot of you away with him if you give him a chance!' cried the fisherman. 'He'll drag you out into the ocean, every one of you!'

'*Heave!*' shouted hairy-chest, ignoring the fisherman. '*Heave*, boys, *heave!*'

And now the gigantic turtle began very slowly to slide up the beach towards the hotel, towards the kitchen, towards the place where the big knives were kept. The womenfolk and the older, fatter, less athletic men followed alongside, shouting encouragement.

'*Heave!*' shouted the hairy-chested anchor-man. 'Put your backs into it, fellers! You can pull harder than that!'

Suddenly, I heard screams. Everyone heard them. They were screams so high-pitched, so shrill and so urgent they cut right through everything. 'No-o-o-o-o!' screamed the scream. 'No! No! No! No! No!'

The crowd froze. The tug-of-war men stopped tugging and the onlookers stopped shouting and every single person present turned towards the place where the screams were coming from.

Half walking, half running down the beach from the hotel, I saw three people, a man, a woman and a small boy. They were half running because the boy was pulling the man along. The man had the boy by the wrist, trying to slow him down, but the boy kept pulling. At the same time, he was jumping and twisting and wriggling and trying to free himself from the father's grip. It was the boy who was screaming.

'Don't!' he screamed. 'Don't do it! Let him go! Please let him go!'

The woman, his mother, was trying to catch hold of the boy's other arm to help restrain him, but the boy was jumping about so much, she didn't succeed.

'Let him go!' screamed the boy. 'It's horrible what you're doing! Please let him go!'

'Stop that, David!' the mother said, still trying to catch his other arm. 'Don't be so childish! You're making a perfect fool of yourself.'

'Daddy!' the boy screamed. 'Daddy! Tell them to let him go!'

'I can't do that, David,' the father said. 'It isn't any of our business.'

The tug-of-war pullers remained motionless, still holding the rope with the gigantic turtle on the end of it. Everyone stood silent and surprised, staring at the boy. They were all a bit off-balance now. They had the slightly hangdog air of people who had been caught doing something that was not entirely honourable.

'Come on now, David,' the father said, pulling against the boy. 'Let's go back to the hotel and leave these people alone.'

'I'm not going back!' the boy shouted. 'I don't want to go back! I want them to let it go!'

'Now, David,' the mother said.

'Beat it, kid,' the hairy-chested man told the boy.

'You're horrible and cruel!' the boy shouted. 'All of you are horrible and cruel!' He threw the words high and shrill at the forty or fifty adults standing there on the beach, and nobody, not even the hairy-chested man, answered him this time. 'Why don't you put him back in the sea?' the boy shouted. 'He hasn't done anything to you! Let him go!'

The father was embarrassed by his son, but he was not ashamed of him. 'He's crazy about animals,' he said, addressing the crowd. 'Back home he's got every kind of animal under the sun. He talks with them.'

'He loves them,' the mother said.

Several people began shuffling their feet around in the sand. Here and there in the crowd it was possible to sense a slight change of mood, a feeling of uneasiness, a touch even of shame. The boy, who could have been no more than eight or nine years old, had stopped struggling with his father now. The father still held him by the wrist, but he was no longer restraining him.

'Go on!' the boy called out. 'Let him go! Undo the rope and let him go!' He stood very small and erect, facing the crowd, his eyes shining like two stars and the wind blowing in his hair. He was magnificent.

'There's nothing we can do, David,' the father said gently. 'Let's go on back.'

'No!' the boy cried out, and at that moment he suddenly gave a twist and wrenched his wrist free from the father's grip. He was away like a streak, running across the sand towards the giant upturned turtle.

'David!' the father yelled, starting after him. 'Stop! Come back!'

The boy dodged and swerved through the crowd like a player running with the ball, and the only person who sprang forward to intercept him was the fisherman. 'Don't you go near that turtle, boy!' he shouted as he made a lunge for the swiftly running figure. But the boy dodged round him and kept going. 'He'll bite you to pieces!' yelled the fisherman. 'Stop, boy! Stop!'

But it was too late to stop him now, and as he came running straight at the turtle's head, the turtle saw him, and the huge upside-down head turned quickly to face him.

The voice of the boy's mother, the stricken, agonized wail of the mother's voice rose up into the evening sky. 'David!' it cried. '*Oh, David!*' And a moment later, the boy was throwing himself on to his knees in the sand and flinging his arms around the wrinkled old neck and hugging the creature to his chest. The boy's cheek was pressing against the turtle's head, and his lips were moving, whispering soft words that nobody else could hear. The turtle became absolutely still. Even the giant flippers stopped waving in the air.

A great sigh, a long soft sigh of relief, went up from the crowd. Many people took a pace or two backwards, as though trying perhaps to get a little further away from something that was beyond their understanding. But the father and mother came forwards together and stood about ten feet away from their son.

'Daddy!' the boy cried out, still caressing the old brown head. 'Please do something, Daddy! Please make them let him go!'

'Can I be of any help here?' said a man in a white suit

who had just come down from the hotel. This, as everyone knew, was Mr Edwards, the manager. He was a tall, beak-nosed Englishman with a long pink face. '*What* an extraordinary thing!' he said, looking at the boy and the turtle. 'He's lucky he hasn't had his head bitten off.' And to the boy he said, 'You'd better come away from there now, sonny. That thing's dangerous.'

'I want them to let him go!' cried the boy, still cradling the head in his arms. 'Tell them to let him go!'

'You realize he could be killed any moment,' the manager said to the boy's father.

'Leave him alone,' the father said.

'Rubbish,' the manager said. 'Go in and grab him. But be quick. And be careful.'

'No,' the father said.

'What do you mean, no?' said the manager. 'These things are lethal! Don't you understand that?'

'Yes,' the father said.

'Then for heaven's sake, man, get him away!' cried the manager. 'There's going to be a very nasty accident if you don't.'

'Who owns it?' the father said. 'Who owns the turtle?'

'We do,' the manager said. 'The hotel has bought it.'

'Then do me a favour,' the father said. 'Let me buy it from you.'

The manager looked at the father, but said nothing.

'You don't know my son,' the father said, speaking quietly. 'He'll go crazy if it's taken up to the hotel and slaughtered. He'll become hysterical.'

'Just pull him away,' the manager said. 'And be quick about it.'

'He loves animals,' the father said. 'He really loves them. He communicates with them.'

The crowd was silent, trying to hear what was being said. Nobody moved away. They stood as though hypnotized.

'If we let it go,' the manager said, 'they'll only catch it again.'

'Perhaps they will,' the father said. 'But those things can swim.'

'I know they can swim,' the manager said. 'They'll catch him all the same. This is a valuable item, you must realize that. The shell alone is worth a lot of money.'

'I don't care about the cost,' the father said. 'Don't worry about that. I want to buy it.'

The boy was still kneeling in the sand beside the turtle, caressing its head.

The manager took a handkerchief from his breast pocket and started wiping his fingers. He was not keen to let the turtle go. He probably had the dinner menu already planned. On the other hand, he didn't want another gruesome accident on his private beach this season. Mr Wasserman and the coconut, he told himself, had been quite enough for one year, thank you very much.

The father said, 'I would deem it a great personal favour, Mr Edwards, if you would let me buy it. And I promise you won't regret it. I'll make quite sure of that.'

The manager's eyebrows went up just a fraction of an inch. He had got the point. He was being offered a bribe. That was a different matter. For a few seconds he went on wiping his hands with the handkerchief. Then he shrugged his shoulders and said, 'Well, I suppose if it will make your boy feel any better . . .'

'Thank you,' the father said.

'Oh, thank you!' the mother cried. 'Thank you so very much!'

'Willy,' the manager said, beckoning to the fisherman.

The fisherman came forwards. He looked thoroughly confused. 'I never seen anything like this before in my whole life,' he said. 'This old turtle was the fiercest I ever caught! He fought like a devil when we brought him in! It took all six of us to land him! That boy's crazy!'

'Yes, I know,' the manager said. 'But now I want you to let him go.'

'Let him go!' the fisherman cried, aghast. 'You mustn't ever let this one go, Mr Edwards! He's broke the record! He's the biggest turtle ever been caught on this island! Easy the biggest! And what about our money?'

'You'll get your money.'

'I got the other five to pay off as well,' the fisherman said, pointing down the beach.

About a hundred yards down, on the water's edge, five black-skinned almost naked men were standing beside a second boat. 'All six of us are in on this, equal shares,' the fisherman went on. 'I can't let him go till we got the money.'

'I guarantee you'll get it,' the manager said. 'Isn't that good enough for you?'

'I'll underwrite that guarantee,' the father of the boy said, stepping forwards. 'And there'll be an extra bonus for all six of the fishermen just as long as you let him go at once. I mean immediately, this instant.'

The fisherman looked at the father. Then he looked at the manager. 'Okay,' he said. 'If that's the way you want it.'

'There's one condition,' the father said. 'Before you get your money, you must promise you won't go straight out and try to catch him again. Not this evening, anyway. Is that understood?'

'Sure,' the fisherman said. 'That's a deal.' He turned and ran down the beach, calling to the other five fishermen. He shouted something to them that we couldn't hear, and in a minute or two, all six of them came back together. Five of them were carrying long thick wooden poles.

The boy was still kneeling beside the turtle's head. 'David,' the father said to him gently. 'It's all right now, David. They're going to let him go.'

The boy looked round, but he didn't take his arms from around the turtle's neck, and he didn't get up. 'When?' he asked.

'Now,' the father said. 'Right now. So you'd better come away.'

'You promise?' the boy said.

'Yes, David, I promise.'

The boy withdrew his arms. He got to his feet. He stepped back a few paces.

'Stand back, everyone!' shouted the fisherman called Willy. 'Stand right back, everybody, please!'

The crowd moved a few yards up the beach. The tug-of-war men let go the rope and moved back with the others.

Willy got down on his hands and knees and crept very cautiously up to one side of the turtle. Then he began untying the knot in the rope. He kept well out of the range of the big flippers as he did this.

When the knot was untied, Willy crawled back. Then the five other fishermen stepped forwards with their poles. The poles were about seven feet long and immensely thick. They wedged them underneath the shell of the turtle and began to rock the great creature from side to side on its shell. The shell had a high dome and was well shaped for rocking.

'Up and down!' sang the fishermen as they rocked away. 'Up and down! Up and down! Up and down!' The old turtle became thoroughly upset, and who could blame it? The big flippers lashed the air frantically, and the head kept shooting in and out of the shell.

'Roll him over!' sang the fishermen. 'Up and over! Roll him over! One more time and over he goes!'

The turtle tilted high up on to its side and crashed down in the sand the right way up.

But it didn't walk away at once. The huge brown head came out and peered cautiously around.

'Go, turtle, go!' the small boy called out. 'Go back to the sea!'

The two hooded black eyes of the turtle peered up at the boy. The eyes were bright and lively, full of the wisdom of great age. The boy looked back at the turtle, and this time when he spoke, his voice was soft and intimate. 'Good-bye, old man,' he said. 'Go far away this time.' The black eyes remained resting on the boy for a few seconds more. Nobody moved. Then, with great dignity, the massive beast turned away and began waddling towards the edge of the ocean. He didn't hurry. He moved sedately over the sandy beach, the big shell rocking gently from side to side as he went.

The crowd watched in silence.

He entered the water.

He kept going.

Soon he was swimming. He was in his element now. He swam gracefully and very fast, with the head held high. The sea was calm, and he made little waves that fanned out behind him on both sides, like the waves of a boat. It was several minutes before we lost sight of him, and by then he was halfway to the horizon.

The guests began wandering back towards the hotel. They were curiously subdued. There was no joking or bantering now, no laughing. Something had happened. Something strange had come fluttering across the beach.

I walked back to my small balcony and sat down with a cigarette. I had an uneasy feeling that this was not the end of the affair.

The next morning at eight o'clock, the Jamaican girl, the one who had told me about Mr Wasserman and the coconut, brought a glass of orange juice to my room.

'Big *big* fuss in the hotel this morning,' she said as she placed the glass on the table and drew back the curtains. 'Everyone flying about all over the place like they was crazy.'

'Why? What's happened?'

'That little boy in number twelve, he's vanished. He disappeared in the night.'

'You mean the turtle boy?'

'That's him,' she said. 'His parents is raising the roof and the manager's going mad.'

'How long's he been missing?'

'About two hours ago his father found his bed empty. But he could've gone any time in the night I reckon.'

'Yes,' I said. 'He could.'

'Everybody in the hotel searching high and low,' she said. 'And a police car just arrived.'

'Maybe he just got up early and went for a climb on the rocks,' I said.

Her large dark haunted-looking eyes rested a moment on my face, then travelled away. 'I do not think so,' she said, and out she went.

I slipped on some clothes and hurried down to the beach. On the beach itself, two native policemen in khaki uniforms were standing with Mr Edwards, the manager. Mr Edwards was doing the talking. The policemen were listening patiently. In the distance, at both ends of the beach, I could see small groups of people, hotel servants as well as hotel guests, spreading out and heading for the rocks. The morning was beautiful. The sky was smoke-blue, faintly glazed with yellow. The sun was up and making diamonds all over the smooth sea. And Mr Edwards was talking loudly to the two native policemen, and waving his arms.

I wanted to help. What should I do? Which way should

I go? It would be pointless simply to follow the others. So I just kept walking towards Mr Edwards.

About then, I saw the fishing-boat. The long wooden canoe with a single mast and a flapping brown sail was still some way out to sea, but it was heading for the beach. The two natives aboard, one at either end, were paddling hard. They were paddling very hard. The paddles rose and fell at such a terrific speed they might have been in a race. I stopped and watched them. Why the great rush to reach the shore? Quite obviously they had something to tell. I kept my eyes on the boat. Over to my left, I could hear Mr Edwards saying to the two policemen, 'It is perfectly ridiculous. I can't have people disappearing just like that from the hotel. You'd better find him fast, you understand me? He's either wandered off somewhere and got lost or he's been kidnapped. Either way, it's the responsibility of the police . . .'

The fishing-boat skimmed over the sea and came gliding up on to the sand at the water's edge. Both men dropped their paddles and jumped out. They started running up the beach. I recognized the one in front as Willy. When he caught sight of the manager and the two policemen, he made straight for them.

'Hey, Mr Edwards!' Willy called out. 'We just seen a crazy thing!'

The manager stiffened and jerked back his neck. The two policemen remained impassive. They were used to excitable people. They met them every day.

Willy stopped in front of the group, his chest heaving in and out with heavy breathing. The other fisherman was close behind him. They were both naked except for a tiny loincloth, their black skins shining with sweat.

'We been paddling full speed for a long way,' Willy said, excusing his out-of-breathness. 'We thought we ought to come back and tell it as quick as we can.'

'Tell what?' the manager said. 'What did you see?'

'It was crazy, man! Absolutely crazy!'

'Get on with it, Willy, for heaven's sake.'

'You won't believe it,' Willy said. 'There ain't nobody going to believe it. Isn't that right, Tom?'

'That's right,' the other fisherman said, nodding vigorously. 'If Willy here hadn't been with me to prove it, I wouldn't have believed it myself!'

'Believed what?' Mr Edwards said. 'Just tell us what you saw.'

'We'd gone off early,' Willy said, 'about four o'clock this morning, and we must've been a couple of miles out before it got light enough to see anything properly. Suddenly, as the sun comes up, we see right ahead of us, not more'n fifty yards away, we see something we couldn't believe not even with our eyes . . .'

'What?' snapped Mr Edwards. 'For heaven's sake get on!'

'We sees that old monster turtle swimming away out there, the one on the beach yesterday, and we sees the boy sitting high up on the turtle's back and riding him over the sea like a horse!'

'You gotta believe it!' the other fisherman cried. 'I sees it too, so you gotta believe it!'

Mr Edwards looked at the two policemen. The two

policemen looked at the fishermen. 'You wouldn't be having us on, would you?' one of the policemen said.

'I swear it!' cried Willy. 'It's the gospel truth! There's this little boy riding high up on the old turtle's back and his feet isn't even touching the water! He's dry as a bone and sitting there comfy and easy as could be! So we go after them. Of course we go after them. At first we try creeping up on them very quietly, like we always do when we're catching a turtle, but the boy sees us. We aren't very far away at this time, you understand. No more than from here to the edge of the water. And when the boy sees us, he sort of leans forwards as if he's saying something to that old turtle, and the turtle's head comes up and he starts swimming like the clappers of hell! Man, could that turtle go! Tom and me can paddle pretty quick when we want to, but we've no chance against that monster! No chance at all! He's going at least twice as fast as we are! Easy twice as fast, what you say, Tom?'

'I'd say he's going *three times* as fast,' Tom said. 'And I'll tell you why. In about ten or fifteen minutes, they're a mile ahead of us.'

'Why on earth didn't you call out to the boy?' the manager asked. 'Why didn't you speak to him earlier on, when you were closer?'

'We never *stop* calling out, man!' Willy cried. 'As soon as the boy sees us and we're not trying to creep up on them any longer, then we start yelling. We yell everything under the sun at that boy to try and get him aboard. "Hey, boy!" I yell at him. "You come on back with us! We'll give you a lift home! That ain't no good what you're doing there, boy! Jump off and swim while you got the chance and we'll pick you up! Go on boy, jump! Your mammy must be waiting for you at home, boy, so why don't you come on in with us?" And once I shouted at him, "Listen, boy! We're gonna make you a promise! We promise not to catch that old turtle if you come with us!"'

'Did he answer you at all?' the manager asked.

'He never even looks round!' Willy said. 'He sits high up on that shell and he's sort of rocking backwards and forwards with his body just like he's urging the old turtle to go faster and faster! You're gonna lose that little boy, Mr Edwards, unless someone gets out there real quick and grabs him away!'

The manager's normally pink face had turned white as paper. 'Which way were they heading?' he asked sharply.

'North,' Willy answered. 'Almost due north.'

'Right!' the manager said. 'We'll take the speed-boat! I want you with us, Willy. And you, Tom.'

The manager, the two policemen and the two fisher-men ran down to where the boat that was used for water-skiing lay beached on the sand. They pushed the boat out, and even the manager lent a hand, wading up to his knees in his well-pressed white trousers. Then they all climbed in.

I watched them go zooming off.

Two hours later, I watched them coming back. They had seen nothing.

All through that day, speed-boats and yachts from other hotels along the coast searched the ocean. In the afternoon, the boy's father hired a helicopter. He rode in it himself and they were up there three hours. They found no trace of the turtle or the boy.

For a week, the search went on, but with no result.

And now, nearly a year has gone by since it happened. In that time, there has been only one significant bit of news. A party of Americans, out from Nassau in the Bahamas, were deep-sea fishing off a large island called Eleuthera. There are literally thousands of coral reefs and small uninhabited islands in this area, and upon one of these tiny islands, the captain of the yacht saw through his binoculars the figure of a small person. There was a sandy beach on the island, and the small person was walking on the beach. The binoculars were passed around, and everyone who looked through them agreed that it was a child of some sort. There was, of course, a lot of excitement on board and the fishing lines were quickly reeled in. The captain steered the yacht straight for the island. When they were half a mile off, they were able, through the binoculars, to see clearly that the figure on the beach was a boy, and although sunburnt, he was almost certainly white-skinned, not a native. At that point, the watchers on the yacht also spotted what looked like a giant turtle on the sand near the boy. What happened next happened very quickly. The boy, who had probably caught sight of the approaching yacht, jumped on the turtle's back and the huge creature entered the water and swam at great speed around the island and out of sight. The yacht searched for two hours, but nothing more was seen either of the boy or the turtle.

There is no reason to disbelieve this report. There were

five people on the yacht. Four of them were Americans and the captain was a Bahamian from Nassau. All of them in turn saw the boy and the turtle through the binoculars.

To reach Eleuthera Island from Jamaica by sea, one must first travel north-east for two hundred and fifty miles and pass through the Windward Passage between Cuba and Haiti. Then one must go north-north-west for a farther three hundred miles at least. This is a total distance of five hundred and fifty miles, which is a very long journey for a small boy to make on the shell of a giant turtle.

Who knows what to think of all this?

One day, perhaps, he will come back, though I personally doubt it. I have a feeling he's quite happy where he is.

Dip in the Pool

First published in *The New Yorker*
(19 January 1952)

On the morning of the third day, the sea calmed. Even the most delicate passengers – those who had not been seen around the ship since sailing time – emerged from their cabins and crept up on to the sun deck, where the deck steward gave them chairs and tucked rugs around their legs and left them lying in rows, their faces upturned to the pale, almost heatless January sun.

It had been moderately rough the first two days, and this sudden calm and the sense of comfort that it brought created a more genial atmosphere over the whole ship. By the time evening came, the passengers, with twelve hours of good weather behind them, were beginning to feel confident, and at eight o'clock that night the main dining-room was filled with people eating and drinking with the assured, complacent air of seasoned sailors.

The meal was not half over when the passengers became aware, by a slight friction between their bodies and the seats of their chairs, that the big ship had actually started rolling again. It was very gentle at first, just a slow, lazy leaning to one side, then to the other, but it was enough to cause a subtle, immediate change of mood over the whole room. A few of the passengers glanced up from their food, hesitating, waiting, almost listening for the next roll, smiling nervously, little secret glimmers of apprehension in their eyes. Some were completely unruffled, some were openly smug, a number of the smug ones making jokes about food and weather in order to torture the few who were beginning to suffer. The movement of the ship then became rapidly more and more violent, and only five or six minutes after the first roll had been noticed, she was swinging heavily from side to side, the passengers bracing themselves in their chairs, leaning against the pull as in a car cornering.

At last the really bad roll came, and Mr William Botibol, sitting at the purser's table, saw his plate of poached turbot with hollandaise sauce sliding suddenly away from under his fork. There was a flutter of excitement, everybody reaching for plates and wine glasses. Mrs Renshaw, seated at the purser's right, gave a little scream and clutched that gentleman's arm.

'Going to be a dirty night,' the purser said, looking at Mrs Renshaw. 'I think it's blowing up a very dirty night.' There was just the faintest suggestion of relish in the way he said it.

A steward came hurrying up and sprinkled water on the tablecloth between the plates. The excitement subsided. Most of the passengers continued with their meal. A small number, including Mrs Renshaw, got carefully to their feet and threaded their ways with a kind of concealed haste between the tables and through the doorway.

'Well,' the purser said, 'there she goes.' He glanced around with approval at the remainder of his flock, who were sitting quiet, looking complacent, their faces reflecting openly that extraordinary pride that travellers seem to take in being recognized as 'good sailors'.

When the eating was finished and the coffee had been served, Mr Botibol, who had been unusually grave and thoughtful since the rolling started, suddenly stood up and carried his cup of coffee around to Mrs Renshaw's vacant place, next to the purser. He seated himself in her chair, then immediately leaned over and began to whisper urgently in the purser's ear. 'Excuse me,' he said, 'but could you tell me something, please?'

The purser, small and fat and red, bent forward to listen. 'What's the trouble. Mr Botibol?'

'What I want to know is this.' The man's face was anxious and the purser was watching it. 'What I want to know is will the captain already have made his estimate on the day's run – you know, for the auction pool? I mean, before it began to get rough like this?'

The purser, who had prepared himself to receive a personal confidence, smiled and leaned back in his seat to relax his full belly. 'I should say so – yes,' he answered. He didn't bother to whisper his reply, although automatically he lowered his voice, as one does when answering a whisperer.

'About how long ago do you think he did it?'

'Some time this afternoon. He usually does it in the afternoon.'

'About what time?'

'Oh, I don't know. Around four o'clock, I should guess.'

'Now tell me another thing. How does the captain

decide which number it shall be? Does he take a lot of trouble over that?'

The purser looked at the anxious frowning face of Mr Botibol and he smiled, knowing quite well what the man was driving at. 'Well, you see, the captain has a little conference with the navigating officer, and they study the weather and a lot of other things, and then they make their estimate.'

Mr Botibol nodded, pondering this answer for a moment. Then he said, 'Do you think the captain knew there was bad weather coming today?'

'I couldn't tell you,' the purser replied. He was looking into the small black eyes of the other man, seeing the two single little sparks of excitement dancing in their centres. 'I really couldn't tell you, Mr Botibol. I wouldn't know.'

'If this gets any worse it might be worth buying some of the low numbers. What do you think?' The whispering was more urgent, more anxious now.

'Perhaps it will,' the purser said. 'I doubt the old man allowed for a really rough night. It was pretty calm this afternoon when he made his estimate.'

The others at the table had become silent and were trying to hear, watching the purser with that intent, half-cocked, listening look that you can see also at the race track when they are trying to overhear a trainer talking about his chance: the slightly open lips, the upstretched eyebrows, the head forward and cocked a little to one side – that desperately straining, half-hypnotized, listening look that comes to all of them when they are hearing something straight from the horse's mouth.

'Now suppose *you* were allowed to buy a number, which one would *you* choose today?' Mr Botibol whispered.

'I don't know what the range is yet,' the purser patiently answered. 'They don't announce the range till the auction starts after dinner. And I'm really not very good at it anyway. I'm only the purser, you know.'

At that point Mr Botibol stood up. 'Excuse me, all,' he said, and he walked carefully away over the swaying floor between the other tables, and twice he had to catch hold of the back of a chair to steady himself against the ship's roll.

'The sun deck, please,' he said to the elevator man.

The wind caught him full in the face as he stepped out on to the open deck. He staggered and grabbed hold of the rail and held on tight with both hands, and he stood there looking out over the darkening sea, where the great waves were welling up high and white horses were riding against the wind with plumes of spray behind them as they went.

'Pretty bad out there, wasn't it, sir?' the elevator man said on the way down.

Mr Botibol was combing his hair back into place with a small red comb. 'Do you think we've slackened speed at all on account of the weather?' he asked.

'Oh my word yes, sir. We slackened off considerable since this started. You got to slacken off speed in weather like this or you'll be throwing the passengers all over the ship.'

Down in the smoking-room people were already gathering for the auction. They were grouping themselves politely around the various tables, the men a little stiff in their dinner-jackets, a little pink and overshaved and stiff beside their cool, white-armed women. Mr Botibol took a chair close to the auctioneer's table. He crossed his legs, folded his arms and settled himself in his seat with the rather desperate air of a man who has made a tremendous decision and refuses to be frightened.

The pool, he was telling himself, would probably be around seven thousand dollars. That was almost exactly what it had been the last two days with the numbers selling for between three and four hundred apiece. It being a British ship, they did it in pounds, but he liked to do his thinking in his own currency. Seven thousand dollars was plenty of money. My goodness yes! And what he would do, he would get them to pay him in hundred-dollar bills and he would take it ashore in the inside pocket of his jacket. No problem there. And right away, yes right away, he would buy a Lincoln convertible. He would pick it up on the way from the ship and drive it home just for the pleasure of seeing Ethel's face when she came out the front door and looked at it. Wouldn't that be something, to see Ethel's face when he glided up to the door in a brand-new pale-green Lincoln convertible! Hello, Ethel honey, he would say, speaking very casual. I just thought I'd get you a little present. I saw it in the window as I went by, so I thought of you and how you were always wanting one. You like it, honey? he would say. You like the colour? And then he would watch her face.

The auctioneer was standing up behind his table now. 'Ladies and gentlemen!' he shouted. 'The captain has estimated the day's run, ending midday tomorrow, at five hundred and fifteen miles. As usual we will take the ten numbers on either side of it to make up the range. That makes it five hundred and five to five hundred and twenty-five. And of course for those who think the true figure will be still farther away, there'll be "low field" and "high field" sold separately as well. Now, we'll draw the first number out of the hat . . . here we are . . . five hundred and twelve?'

The room became quiet. The people sat still in their chairs, all eyes watching the auctioneer. There was a certain tension in the air, and as the bids got higher, the tension grew. This wasn't a game or a joke; you could be sure of that by the way one man would look across at another who had raised his bid – smiling perhaps, but only the lips smiling, the eyes bright and absolutely cold.

Number five hundred and twelve was knocked down for one hundred and ten pounds. The next three or four numbers fetched roughly the same amount.

The ship was rolling heavily, and each time she went over, the wooden panelling on the walls creaked as if it were going to split. The passengers held on to the arms of their chairs, concentrating upon the auction.

'Low field!' the auctioneer called out. 'The next number is low field.'

Mr Botibol sat up very straight and tense. He would wait, he had decided, until the others had finished bidding, then he would jump in and make the last bid. He had figured that there must be at least five hundred dollars in his account at the bank at home, probably nearer six. That was about two hundred pounds – over two hundred. This ticket wouldn't fetch more than that.

'As you all know,' the auctioneer was saying, 'low field covers every number *below* the smallest number in the range, in this case every number below five hundred and five. So, if you think this ship is going to cover less than five hundred and five miles in the twenty-four hours ending at noon tomorrow, you better get in and buy this number. So what am I bid?'

It went clear up to one hundred and thirty pounds. Others besides Mr Botibol seemed to have noticed that the weather was rough. One hundred and forty ... fifty ... There it stopped. The auctioneer raised his hammer.

'Going at one hundred and fifty ...'

'Sixty!' Mr Botibol called, and every face in the room turned and looked at him.

'Seventy!'

'Eighty!' Mr Botibol called.

'Ninety!'

'Two hundred!' Mr Botibol called. He wasn't stopping now – for anyone.

There was a pause.

'Any advance on two hundred pounds?'

Sit still, he told himself. Sit absolutely still and don't look up. Hold your breath. No one's going to bid you up so long as you hold your breath.

'Going for two hundred pounds ...' The auctioneer

had a pink bald head and there were little beads of sweat sparkling on top of it. 'Going . . .' Mr Botibol held his breath. 'Going . . . Gone!' The man banged the hammer on the table. Mr Botibol wrote out a cheque and handed it to the auctioneer's assistant, then he settled back in his chair to wait for the finish. He did not want to go to bed before he knew how much there was in the pool.

They added it up after the last number had been sold and it came to twenty-one hundred-odd pounds. That was around six thousand dollars. Ninety per cent to go to the winner, ten per cent to seamen's charities. Ninety per cent of six thousand was five thousand four hundred. Well – that was enough. He could buy the Lincoln convertible and there would be something left over, too. With this gratifying thought, he went off, happy and excited, to his cabin.

When Mr Botibol awoke the next morning he lay quite still for several minutes with his eyes shut, listening for the sound of the gale, waiting for the roll of the ship. There was no sound of any gale and the ship was not rolling. He jumped up and peered out of the porthole. The sea – Oh Jesus God – was smooth as glass, the great ship was moving through it fast, obviously making up for time lost during the night. Mr Botibol turned away and sat slowly down on the edge of his bunk. A fine electricity of fear was beginning to prickle under the skin of his stomach. He hadn't a hope now. One of the higher numbers was certain to win it after this.

'Oh my God,' he said aloud. 'What shall I do?'

What, for example, would Ethel say? It was simply not possible to tell her that he had spent almost all of their two years' savings on a ticket in the ship's pool. Nor was it possible to keep the matter secret. To do that he would have to tell her to stop drawing cheques. And what about the monthly instalments on the television set and the Encyclopaedia Britannica? Already he could see the anger and contempt in the woman's eyes, the blue becoming grey and the eyes themselves narrowing as they always did when there was anger in them.

'Oh my God. What *shall* I do?'

There was no point in pretending that he had the slightest chance now – not unless the goddam ship started to go backwards. They'd have to put her in reverse and go full speed astern and keep right on going if he was to have any chance of winning it now. Well, maybe he should ask the captain to do just that. Offer him ten per cent of the profits. Offer him more if he wanted it. Mr Botibol started to giggle. Then very suddenly he stopped, his eyes and mouth both opening wide in a kind of shocked surprise. For it was at this moment that the idea came. It hit him hard and quick, and he jumped up from his bed, terribly excited, ran over to the porthole and looked out again. Well, he thought, why not? Why ever not? The sea was calm and he wouldn't have any trouble keeping afloat until they picked him up. He had a vague feeling that someone had done this thing before, but that didn't prevent him from doing it again. The ship would have to stop and lower a boat, and the boat would have to go back maybe half a mile to get him, and then it would have to return to the ship and be hoisted back on board. It would take at least an hour, the whole thing. An hour was about thirty miles. It would knock thirty miles off the day's run. That would do it. 'Low field' would be sure to win it then. Just so long as he made certain someone saw him falling over; but that would be simple to arrange. And he'd better wear light clothes, something easy to swim in. Sports clothes, that was it. He would dress as though he were going up to play some deck tennis – just a shirt and a pair of shorts and tennis shoes. And leave his watch behind. What was the time? Nine fifteen. The sooner the better, then. Do it now and get it over with. Have to do it soon, because the time limit was midday.

Mr Botibol was both frightened and excited when he stepped out on to the sun deck in his sports clothes. His small body was wide at the hips, tapering upward to extremely narrow sloping shoulders, so that it resembled, in shape at any rate, a bollard. His white skinny legs were covered with black hairs, and he came cautiously out on deck, treading softly in his tennis shoes. Nervously he looked around him. There was only one other person in sight, an elderly woman with very thick ankles and immense buttocks, who was leaning over the rail staring at the sea. She was wearing a coat of Persian lamb and the collar was turned up so Mr Botibol couldn't see her face.

He stood still, examining her carefully from a distance. Yes, he told himself, she would probably do. She would probably give the alarm just as quickly as anyone else. But wait one minute, take your time, William Botibol, take your time. Remember what you told yourself a few minutes ago in the cabin when you were changing? You remember that?

The thought of leaping off a ship into the ocean a thousand miles from the nearest land had made Mr Botibol – a cautious man at the best of times – unusually advertent. He was by no means satisfied yet that this woman he saw before him was *absolutely certain* to give the alarm when he made his jump. In his opinion there were two possible reasons why she might fail him. Firstly, she might be deaf and blind. It was not very probable, but on the other hand it *might* be so, and why take a chance? All he had to do was check it by talking to her for a moment beforehand. Secondly – and this will demonstrate how suspicious the mind of a man can become when it is working through self-preservation and fear – secondly, it had occurred to him that the woman might herself be the owner of one of the high numbers in the pool and as such would have a sound financial reason for not wishing to stop the ship. Mr Botibol recalled that people had killed their fellows for far less than six thousand dollars. It was happening every day in the newspapers. So why take a chance on that either? Check on it first. Be sure of your facts. Find out about it by a little polite conversation. Then, provided that the woman appeared also to be a pleasant, kindly human being, the thing was a cinch and he could leap overboard with a light heart.

Mr Botibol advanced casually towards the woman and took up a position beside her, leaning on the rail. 'Hullo,' he said pleasantly.

She turned and smiled at him, a surprisingly lovely, almost a beautiful smile, although the face itself was very plain. 'Hullo,' she answered him.

Check, Mr Botibol told himself, on the first question. She is neither blind nor deaf. 'Tell me,' he said, coming straight to the point, 'what did you think of the auction last night?'

'Auction?' she asked, frowning. 'Auction? What auction?'

'You know, that silly old thing they have in the lounge after dinner, selling numbers on the ship's daily run. I just wondered what you thought about it.'

She shook her head, and again she smiled, a sweet and pleasant smile that had in it perhaps the trace of an apology. 'I'm very lazy,' she said. 'I always go to bed early. I have my dinner in bed. It's so restful to have dinner in bed.'

Mr Botibol smiled back at her and began to edge away. 'Got to go and get my exercise now,' he said. 'Never miss my exercise in the morning. It was nice seeing you. Very nice seeing you . . .' He retreated about ten paces, and the woman let him go without looking around.

Everything was now in order. The sea was calm, he was lightly dressed for swimming, there were almost certainly no man-eating sharks in this part of the Atlantic, and there was this pleasant kindly old woman to give the alarm. It was a question now only of whether the ship would be delayed long enough to swing the balance in his favour. Almost certainly it would. In any event, he could do a little to help in that direction himself. He could make a few difficulties about getting hauled up into the lifeboat. Swim around a bit, back away from them surreptitiously as they tried to come up close to fish him out. Every minute, every second gained would help him win. He began to move forward again to the rail, but now a new fear assailed him. Would he get caught in the propeller? He had heard about that happening to persons falling off the sides of big ships. But then, he wasn't going to fall, he was going to jump, and that was a very different thing. Provided he jumped out far enough he would be sure to clear the propeller.

Mr Botibol advanced slowly to a position at the rail about twenty yards away from the woman. She wasn't looking at him now. So much the better. He didn't want her watching him as he jumped off. So long as no one was watching he would be able to say afterwards that he had slipped and fallen by accident. He peered over the side of the ship. It was a long, long drop. Come to think of it now, he might easily hurt himself badly if he hit the water flat. Wasn't there someone who once split his stomach open that way, doing a belly flop from a high dive? He must jump straight and land feet first. Go in like a knife. Yes, sir. The water seemed cold and deep and grey and it made him shiver to look at it. But it was now or never. Be a man, William Botibol, be a man. All right then . . . now . . . here goes . . .

He climbed up on to the wide wooden toprail, stood there poised, balancing for three terrifying seconds, then he leaped – he leaped up and out as far as he could go and at the same time he shouted, '*Help!*'

'*Help! Help!*' he shouted as he fell. Then he hit the water and went under.

When the first shout for help sounded, the woman who was leaning on the rail started up and gave a little jump of surprise. She looked around quickly and saw sailing past her through the air this small man dressed in white shorts and tennis shoes, spread-eagled and shouting as he went. For a moment she looked as though she weren't quite sure what she ought to do: throw a life belt, run away and give the alarm, or simply turn and yell. She drew back a pace from the rail and swung half round facing up to the bridge, and for this brief moment she remained motionless, tense, undecided. Then almost at once she seemed to relax, and she leaned forward far over the rail, staring at the water, where it was turbulent in the ship's wake. Soon a tiny round black head appeared in the foam, an arm was raised about it, once, twice, vigorously waving, and a small faraway voice was heard calling something that was difficult to understand. The woman leaned still farther over the rail, trying to keep the little bobbing black speck in sight, but soon, so very soon, it was such a long way away that she couldn't even be sure it was there at all.

After a while another woman came out on deck. This one was bony and angular, and she wore horn-rimmed spectacles. She spotted the first woman and walked over to her, treading the deck in the deliberate, military fashion of all spinsters.

'So *there* you are,' she said.

The woman with the fat ankles turned and looked at her, but said nothing.

'I've been searching for you,' the bony one continued. 'Searching all over.'

'It's very odd,' the woman with the fat ankles said. 'A man dived overboard just now, with his clothes on.'

'Nonsense!'

'Oh yes. He said he wanted to get some exercise and he dived in and didn't even bother to take his clothes off.'

'You better come down now,' the bony woman said. Her mouth had suddenly become firm, her whole face sharp and alert, and she spoke less kindly than before. 'And don't you ever go wandering about on deck alone like this again. You know quite well you're meant to wait for me.'

'Yes, Maggie,' the woman with the fat ankles answered, and again she smiled, a tender, trusting smile, and she took the hand of the other one and allowed herself to be led away across the deck.

'Such a nice man,' she said. 'He waved to me.'

William and Mary

First published in *Kiss Kiss* (1960)

William Pearl did not leave a great deal of money when he died, and his will was a simple one. With the exception of a few small bequests to relatives, he left all his property to his wife.

The solicitor and Mrs Pearl went over it together in the solicitor's office, and when the business was completed, the widow got up to leave. At that point, the solicitor took a sealed envelope from the folder on his desk and held it out to his client.

'I have been instructed to give you this,' he said. 'Your husband sent it to us shortly before he passed away.' The solicitor was pale and prim, and out of respect for a widow he kept his head on one side as he spoke, looking downwards. 'It appears that it might be something personal, Mrs Pearl. No doubt you'd like to take it home with you and read it in privacy.'

Mrs Pearl accepted the envelope and went out into the street. She paused on the pavement, feeling the thing with her fingers. A letter of farewell from William? Probably, yes. A formal letter. It was bound to be formal – stiff and formal. The man was incapable of acting otherwise. He had never done anything informal in his life.

My dear Mary, I trust that you will not permit my departure from this world to upset you too much, but that you will continue to

observe those precepts which have guided you so well during our
partnership together. Be diligent and dignified in all things. Be
thrifty with your money. Be very careful that you do not . . . et
cetera, et cetera.

A typical William letter.

Or was it possible that he might have broken down at
the last moment and written her something beautiful?
Maybe this was a beautiful tender message, a sort of love
letter, a lovely warm note of thanks to her for giving him
thirty years of her life and for ironing a million shirts and
cooking a million meals and making a million beds, something that she could read over and over again, once a day
at least, and she would keep it for ever in the box on her
dressing-table together with her brooches.

There is no knowing what people will do when they are
about to die, Mrs Pearl told herself, and she tucked the
envelope under her arm and hurried home.

She let herself in the front door and went straight to
the living-room and sat down on the sofa without removing her hat or coat. Then she opened the envelope and
drew out the contents. These consisted, she saw, of some
fifteen or twenty sheets of lined white paper, folded over
once and held together at the top left-hand corner by a
clip. Each sheet was covered with the small, neat, forward-
sloping writing that she knew so well, but when she noticed
how much of it there was, and in what a neat businesslike
manner it was written, and how the first page didn't even
begin in the nice way a letter should, she began to get
suspicious.

She looked away. She lit herself a cigarette. She took one puff and laid the cigarette in the ashtray.

If this is about what I am beginning to suspect it is about, she told herself, then I don't want to read it.

Can one refuse to read a letter from the dead?

Yes.

Well . . .

She glanced over at William's empty chair on the other side of the fireplace. It was a big brown leather armchair, and there was a depression on the seat of it, made by his buttocks over the years. Higher up, on the backrest, there was a dark oval stain on the leather where his head had rested. He used to sit reading in that chair and she would be opposite him on the sofa, sewing on buttons or mending socks or putting a patch on the elbow of one of his jackets, and every now and then a pair of eyes would glance up from the book and settle on her, watchful, but strangely impersonal, as if calculating something. She had never liked those eyes. They were ice blue, cold, small, and rather close together, with two deep vertical lines of disapproval dividing them. All her life they had been watching her. And even now, after a week alone in the house, she sometimes had an uneasy feeling that they were still there, following her around, staring at her from doorways, from empty chairs, through a window at night.

Slowly she reached into her handbag and took out her spectacles and put them on. Then, holding the pages up high in front of her so that they caught the late afternoon light from the window behind, she started to read:

This note, my dear Mary, is entirely for you, and will be given you shortly after I am gone.

Do not be alarmed by the sight of all this writing. It is nothing but an attempt on my part to explain to you precisely what Landy is going to do to me, and why I have agreed that he should do it, and what are his theories and his hopes. You are my wife and you have a right to know these things. In fact you must *know them. During the past few days I have tried very hard to speak with you about Landy, but you have steadfastly refused to give me a hearing. This, as I have already told you, is a very foolish attitude to take, and I find it not entirely an unselfish one either. It stems mostly from ignorance, and I am absolutely convinced that if only you were made aware of all the facts, you would immediately change your view. That is why I am hoping that when I am no longer with you, and your mind is less distracted, you will consent to listen to me more carefully through these pages. I swear to you that when you have read my story, your sense of antipathy will vanish, and enthusiasm will take its place. I even dare to hope that you will become a little proud of what I have done.*

As you read on, you must forgive me, if you will, for the coolness of my style, but this is the only way I know of getting my message over to you clearly. You see, as my time draws near, it is natural that I begin to brim with every kind of sentimentality under the sun. Each day I grow more extravagantly wistful, especially in the evenings, and unless I watch myself closely my emotions will be overflowing on to these pages.

I have a wish, for example, to write something about you and what a satisfactory wife you have been to me through the years, and I am promising myself that if there is time, and I still have the strength, I shall do that next.

I have a yearning also to speak about this Oxford of mine where I have been living and teaching for the past seventeen years, to tell something about the glory of the place and to explain, if I can, a little of what it has meant to have been allowed to work in its midst. All the things and places that I loved so well keep crowding in on me now in this gloomy bedroom. They are bright and beautiful as they always were, and today, for some reason, I can see them more clearly than ever. The path around the lake in the gardens of Worcester College, where Lovelace used to walk. The gateway at Pembroke. The view westward over the town from Magdalen Tower. The great hall at Christ Church. The little rockery at St John's where I have counted more than a dozen varieties of campanula, including the rare and dainty C. waldsteiniana. But there, you see! I haven't even begun and already I'm falling into the trap. So let me get started now; and let you read it slowly, my dear, without any of that sense of sorrow or disapproval that might otherwise embarrass your understanding. Promise me now that you will read it slowly, and that you will put yourself in a cool and patient frame of mind before you begin.

The details of the illness that struck me down so suddenly in my middle life are known to you. I need not waste time upon them — except to admit at once how foolish I was not to have gone earlier to my doctor. Cancer is one of the few remaining diseases that these modern drugs cannot cure. A surgeon can operate if it has not spread too far; but with me, not only did I leave it too late, but the thing had the effrontery to attack me in the pancreas, making both surgery and survival equally impossible.

So here I was with somewhere between one and six months left to live, growing more melancholy every hour — and then, all of a sudden, in comes Landy.

That was six weeks ago, on a Tuesday morning, very early, long before your visiting time, and the moment he entered I knew there was some sort of madness in the wind. He didn't creep in on his toes, sheepish and embarrassed, not knowing what to say, like all my other visitors. He came in strong and smiling, and he strode up to the bed and stood there looking down at me with a wild bright glimmer in his eyes, and he said, 'William, my boy, this is perfect. You're just the one I want!'

Perhaps I should explain to you here that although John Landy has never been to our house, and you have seldom if ever met him, I myself have been friendly with him for at least nine years. I am, of course, primarily a teacher of philosophy, but as you know I've lately been dabbling a good deal in psychology as well. Landy's interests and mine have therefore slightly overlapped. He is a magnificent neurosurgeon, one of the finest, and recently he has been kind enough to let me study the results of some of his work, especially the varying effects of prefrontal lobotomies upon different types of psychopath. So you can see that when he suddenly burst in on me Tuesday morning, we were by no means strangers to one another.

'Look,' he said, pulling up a chair beside the bed. 'In a few weeks you're going to be dead. Correct?'

Coming from Landy, the question didn't seem especially unkind. In a way it was refreshing to have a visitor brave enough to touch upon the forbidden subject.

'You're going to expire right here in this room, and then they'll take you out and cremate you.'

'Bury me,' I said.

'That's even worse. And then what? Do you believe you'll go to heaven?'

'I doubt it,' I said, 'though it would be comforting to think so.'

'Or hell, perhaps?'

'I don't really see why they should send me there.'

'You never know, my dear William.'

'What's all this about?' I asked.

'Well,' he said, and I could see him watching me carefully, 'personally, I don't believe that after you're dead you'll ever hear of yourself again – unless . . .' and here he paused and smiled and leaned closer '. . . unless, of course, you have the sense to put yourself into my hands. Would you care to consider a proposition?'

The way he was staring at me, and studying me, and appraising me with a queer kind of hungriness, I might have been a piece of prime beef on the counter and he had bought it and was waiting for them to wrap it up.

'I'm really serious about it, William. Would you care to consider a proposition?'

'I don't know what you're talking about.'

'Then listen and I'll tell you. Will you listen to me?'

'Go on then, if you like. I doubt I've got very much to lose by hearing it.'

'On the contrary, you have a great deal to gain – especially after you're dead.'

I am sure he was expecting me to jump when he said this, but for some reason I was ready for it. I lay quite still, watching his face and that slow white smile of his that always revealed the gold clasp of an upper denture curled round the canine on the left side of his mouth.

'This is a thing, William, that I've been working on quietly for some years. One or two others here at the hospital have been helping me, especially Morrison, and we've completed a number of fairly successful trials with laboratory animals. I'm at the stage now where I'm ready to have a go with a man. It's a big idea, and it may sound a bit far-fetched at first, but from a surgical point of view there doesn't seem to be any reason why it shouldn't be more or less practicable.'

Landy leaned forward and placed both his hands on the edge of my bed. He has a good face, handsome in a bony sort of way, and with none of the usual doctor's look about it. You know that look, most of them have it. It glimmers at you out of their eyeballs like a dull electric sign and it reads ONLY I CAN SAVE YOU. But John Landy's eyes were wide and bright and little sparks of excitement were dancing in the centres of them.

'Quite a long time ago,' he said, 'I saw a short medical film that had been brought over from Russia. It was a rather gruesome thing, but interesting. It showed a dog's head completely severed from the body, but with the normal blood supply being maintained through the arteries and veins by means of an artificial heart. Now the thing is this: that dog's head, sitting there all alone on a sort of tray, was alive. The brain was functioning. They proved it by several tests. For example, when food was smeared on the dog's lips, the tongue would come out and lick it away; and the eyes would follow a person moving across the room.

'It seemed reasonable to conclude from this that the head and the brain did not need to be attached to the rest of the body in order to remain alive – provided, of course, that a supply of properly oxygenated blood could be maintained.

'Now then. My own thought, which grew out of seeing this film, was to remove the brain from the skull of a human and keep it alive and functioning as an independent unit for an *unlimited period after he is dead.* Your *brain, for example, after* you *are dead.'*

'I don't like that,' I said.

'Don't interrupt, William. Let me finish. So far as I can tell from subsequent experiments, the brain is a peculiarly self-supporting object. It manufactures its own cerebrospinal fluid. The magic processes of thought and memory which go on inside it are manifestly not impaired by the absence of limbs or trunk or even of skull, provided, as I say, that you keep pumping in the right kind of oxygenated blood under the proper conditions.

'My dear William, just think for a moment of your own brain. It is in perfect shape. It is crammed full of a lifetime of learning. It has taken you years of work to make it what it is. It is just beginning to give out some first-rate original ideas. Yet soon it is going to have to die along with the rest of your body simply because your silly little pancreas is lousy with cancer.'

'No thank you,' I said to him. 'You can stop there. It's a repulsive idea, and even if you could do it, which I doubt, it would be quite pointless. What possible use is there in keeping my brain alive if I couldn't talk or see or hear or feel? Personally, I can think of nothing more unpleasant.'

'I believe that you would be able to communicate with us,' Landy said. 'And we might even succeed in giving you a certain amount of vision. But let's take this slowly. I'll come to all that later on. The fact remains that you're going to die fairly soon whatever happens; and my plans would not involve touching you at all until *after* you are dead. Come now, William. No true philosopher could object to lending his dead body to the cause of science.'

'That's not putting it quite straight,' I answered. 'It seems to me there'd be some doubt as to whether I were dead or alive by the time you'd finished with me.'

'Well,' he said, smiling a little, 'I suppose you're right about that. But I don't think you ought to turn me down quite so quickly, before you know a bit more about it.'

'I said I don't want to hear it.'

'Have a cigarette,' he said, holding out his case.

'I don't smoke, you know that.'

He took one himself and lit it with a tiny silver lighter that was no bigger than a shilling piece. 'A present from the people who make my instruments,' he said. 'Ingenious, isn't it?'

I examined the lighter, then handed it back.

'May I go on?' he asked.

'I'd rather you didn't.'

'Just lie still and listen. I think you'll find it quite interesting.'

There were some blue grapes on a plate beside my bed. I put the plate on my chest and began eating the grapes.

'At the very moment of death,' Landy said, 'I should have to be standing by so that I could step in immediately and try to keep your brain alive.'

'You mean leaving it in the head?'

'To start with, yes. I'd have to.'

'And where would you put it after that?'

'If you want to know, in a sort of basin.'

'Are you really serious about this?'

'Certainly I'm serious.'

'All right. Go on.'

'I suppose you know that when the heart stops and the brain is deprived of fresh blood and oxygen, its tissues die very rapidly.

193

Anything from four to six minutes and the whole thing's dead. Even after three minutes you may get a certain amount of damage. So I should have to work rapidly to prevent this from happening. But with the help of the machine, it should all be quite simple.'

'What machine?'

'The artificial heart. We've got a nice adaptation here of the one originally devised by Alexis Carrel and Lindbergh. It oxygenates the blood, keeps it at the right temperature, pumps it in at the right pressure, and does a number of other little necessary things. It's really not at all complicated.'

'Tell me what you would do at the moment of death,' I said. 'What is the first thing you would do?'

'Do you know anything about the vascular and venous arrangements of the brain?'

'No.'

'Then listen. It's not difficult. The blood supply to the brain is derived from two main sources, the internal carotid arteries and the vertebral arteries. There are two of each, making four arteries in all. Got that?'

'Yes.'

'And the return system is even simpler. The blood is drained away by only two large veins, the internal jugulars. So you have four arteries going up – they go up the neck, of course – and two veins coming down. Around the brain itself they naturally branch out into other channels, but those don't concern us. We never touch them.'

'All right,' I said. 'Imagine that I've just died. Now what would you do?'

'I should immediately open your neck and locate the four arteries, the carotids and the vertebrals. I should then perfuse them, which means that I'd stick a large hollow needle into each. These four needles would be connected by tubes to the artificial heart.

'Then, working quickly, I would dissect out both the left and right internal jugular veins and hitch these also to the heart machine to complete the circuit. Now switch on the machine, which is already primed with the right type of blood, and there you are. The circulation through your brain would be restored.'

'I'd be like that Russian dog.'

'I don't think you would. For one thing, you'd certainly lose consciousness when you died, and I very much doubt whether you would come to again for quite a long time – if indeed you came to at all. But, conscious or not, you'd be in a rather interesting position, wouldn't you? You'd have a cold dead body and a living brain.'

Landy paused to savour this delightful prospect. The man was so entranced and bemused by the whole idea that he evidently found it impossible to believe I might not be feeling the same way.

'We could now afford to take our time,' he said. 'And believe me, we'd need it. The first thing we'd do would be to wheel you to the operating-room, accompanied of course by the machine, which must never stop pumping. The next problem . . .'

'All right,' I said. 'That's enough. I don't have to hear the details.'

'Oh but you must,' he said. 'It is important that you should know precisely what is going to happen to you all the way through. You see, afterwards, when you regain consciousness, it will be much more satisfactory from your point of view if you are able to *remember exactly* where *you are and* how *you came to be there. If only for your own peace of mind you should know that. You agree?'*

I lay still on the bed, watching him.

'So the next problem would be to remove your brain, intact and undamaged, from your dead body. The body is useless. In fact it has already started to decay. The skull and the face are also useless. They are both encumbrances and I don't want them around. All I want is the brain, the clean beautiful brain, alive and perfect. So when I get you on the table I will take a saw, a small oscillating saw, and with this I shall proceed to remove the whole vault of your skull. You'd still be unconscious at that point so I wouldn't have to bother with anaesthetic.'

'Like hell you wouldn't,' I said.

'You'd be out cold, I promise you that, William. Don't forget you died just a few minutes before.'

'Nobody's sawing off the top of my skull without an anaesthetic,' I said.

Landy shrugged his shoulders. 'It makes no difference to me,' he said. 'I'll be glad to give you a little procaine if you want it. If it will make you any happier I'll infiltrate the whole scalp with procaine, the whole head, from the neck up.'

'Thanks very much,' I said.

'You know,' he went on, 'it's extraordinary what sometimes happens. Only last week a man was brought in unconscious, and I opened his head without any anaesthetic at all and removed a small blood clot. I was still working inside the skull when he woke up and began talking.

'"Where am I?" he asked.

'"You're in hospital."'

'"Well," he said. "Fancy that."

'"Tell me," I asked him, "is this bothering you, what I'm doing?"

'"No," he answered. "Not at all. What are you doing?"

'"I'm just removing a blood clot from your brain."

'"You are?"

'"Just lie still. Don't move. I'm nearly finished."

'"So that's the bastard been giving me all those headaches," the man said.'

Landy paused and smiled, remembering the occasion. 'That's word for word what the man said,' he went on, 'although the next day he couldn't even recollect the incident. It's a funny thing, the brain.'

'I'll have the procaine,' I said.

'As you wish, William. And now, as I say, I'd take a small oscillating saw and carefully remove your complete calvarium — the whole vault of the skull. This would expose the top half of the brain, or rather the outer covering in which it is wrapped. You may or may not know that there are three separate coverings round the brain itself — the outer one called the dura mater or dura, the middle one called the arachnoid, and the inner one called the pia mater or pia. Most laymen seem to have the idea that the brain is a naked thing floating around in fluid in your head. But it isn't. It's wrapped up neatly in these three strong coverings, and the cerebrospinal fluid actually flows within the little gap between the two inner coverings, known as the subarachnoid space. As I told you before, this fluid is manufactured by the brain, and it drains off into the venous system by osmosis.

'I myself would leave all three coverings — don't they have lovely names, the dura, the arachnoid, and the pia? — I'd leave them all intact. There are many reasons for this, not least among them being the fact that within the dura run the venous channels that drain the blood from the brain into the jugular.

'Now,' he went on, 'we've got the upper half of your skull off so that the top of the brain, wrapped in its outer covering, is exposed. The next step is the really tricky one: to release the whole package so that it can be lifted cleanly away, leaving the stubs of the four supply arteries and the two veins hanging underneath ready to be re-connected to the machine. This is an immensely lengthy and complicated business involving the delicate chipping away of much bone, the severing of many nerves, and the cutting and tying of numerous blood vessels. The only way I could do it with any hope of success would be by taking a rongeur and slowly biting off the rest of your skull, peeling it off downwards like an orange until the sides and underneath of the brain covering are fully exposed. The problems involved are highly technical and I won't go into them, but I feel fairly sure that the work can be done. It's simply a question of surgical skill and patience. And don't forget that I'd have plenty of time, as much as I wanted, because the artificial heart would be continually pumping away alongside the operating-table, keeping the brain alive.

'Now, let's assume that I've succeeded in peeling off your skull and removing everything else that surrounds the sides of the brain. That leaves it connected to the body only at the base, mainly by the spinal column and by the two large veins and the four arteries that are supplying it with blood. So what next?

'I would sever the spinal column just above the first cervical vertebra, taking great care not to harm the two vertebral arteries which are in that area. But you must remember that the dura or outer covering is open at this place to receive the spinal column, so

I'd have to close this opening by sewing the edges of the dura together. There'd be no problem there.

'At this point, I would be ready for the final move. To one side, on a table, I'd have a basin of a special shape, and this would be filled with what we call Ringer's Solution. That is a special kind of fluid we use for irrigation in neurosurgery. I would now cut the brain completely loose by severing the supply arteries and the veins. Then I would simply pick it up in my hands and transfer it to the basin. This would be the only other time during the whole proceeding when the blood flow would be cut off; but once it was in the basin, it wouldn't take a moment to re-connect the stubs of the arteries and veins to the artificial heart.

'So there you are,' Landy said. 'Your brain is now in the basin, and still alive, and there isn't any reason why it shouldn't stay alive for a very long time, years and years perhaps, provided we looked after the blood and the machine.'

'But would it function?'

'My dear William, how should I know? I can't even tell you whether it would ever regain consciousness.'

'And if it did?'

'There now! That would be fascinating!'

'Would it?' I said, and I must admit I had my doubts.

'Of course it would! Lying there with all your thinking processes working beautifully, and your memory as well . . .'

'And not being able to see or feel or smell or hear or talk,' I said.

'Ah!' he cried. 'I knew I'd forgotten something! I never told you about the eye. Listen. I am going to try to leave one of your optic nerves intact, as well as the eye itself. The optic nerve is a little thing about the thickness of a clinical thermometer and about two inches in length as it stretches between the brain and the eye. The beauty of it is that it's not really a nerve at all. It's an outpouching of the brain itself, and the dura or brain covering extends along it and is attached to the eyeball. The back of the eye is therefore in very close contact with the brain, and cerebrospinal fluid flows right up to it.

'All this suits my purpose very well, and makes it reasonable to suppose that I could succeed in preserving one of your eyes. I've already constructed a small plastic case to contain the eyeball, instead of your own socket, and when the brain is in the basin, submerged in Ringer's Solution, the eyeball in its case will float on the surface of the liquid.'

'Staring at the ceiling,' I said.

'I suppose so, yes. I'm afraid there wouldn't be any muscles there to move it around. But it might be sort of fun to lie there so quietly and comfortably peering out at the world from your basin.'

'Hilarious,' I said. 'How about leaving me an ear as well?'

'I'd rather not try an ear this time.'

'I want an ear,' I said. 'I insist upon an ear.'

'No.'

'I want to listen to Bach.'

'You don't understand how difficult it would be,' Landy said gently. 'The hearing apparatus — the cochlea, as it's called — is a far more delicate mechanism than the eye. What's more, it is encased in bone. So is a part of the auditory nerve that connects it with the brain. I couldn't possibly chisel the whole thing out intact.'

'Couldn't you leave it encased in the bone and bring the bone to the basin?'

'No,' he said firmly. 'This thing is complicated enough already. And anyway, if the eye works, it doesn't matter all that much about your hearing. We can always hold up messages for you to read. You really must leave me to decide what is possible and what isn't.'

'I haven't yet said that I'm going to do it.'

'I know, William, I know.'

'I'm not sure I fancy the idea very much.'

'Would you rather be dead, altogether?'

'Perhaps I would. I don't know yet. I wouldn't be able to talk, would I?'

'Of course not.'

'Then how would I communicate with you? How would you know that I'm conscious?'

'It would be easy for us to know whether or not you regain consciousness,' Landy said. 'The ordinary electroencephalograph could tell us that. We'd attach the electrodes directly to the frontal lobes of your brain, there in the basin.'

'And you could actually tell?'

'Oh, definitely. Any hospital could do that part of it.'

'But I couldn't communicate with you.'

'As a matter of fact,' Landy said, 'I believe you could. There's a man up in London called Wertheimer who's doing some interesting work on the subject of thought communication, and I've been in touch with him. You know, don't you, that the thinking brain throws off electrical and chemical discharges? And that these discharges go out in the form of waves, rather like radio waves?'

'I know a bit about it,' I said.

'Well, Wertheimer has constructed an apparatus somewhat similar to the encephalograph, though far more sensitive, and he maintains that within certain narrow limits it can help him to interpret the actual things that a brain is thinking. It produces a kind of graph which is apparently decipherable into words or thoughts. Would you like me to ask Wertheimer to come and see you?'

'No,' I said. Landy was already taking it for granted that I was going to go through with this business, and I resented his attitude. Go away now and leave me alone,' I told him. 'You won't get anywhere by trying to rush me.'

He stood up at once and crossed to the door.

'One question,' I said.

He paused with a hand on the doorknob. 'Yes, William?'

'Simply this. Do you yourself honestly believe that when my brain is in that basin, my mind will be able to function exactly as it is doing at present? Do you believe that I will be able to think and reason as I can now? And will the power of memory remain?'

'I don't see why not,' he answered. 'It's the same brain. It's alive. It's undamaged. In fact, it's completely untouched. We haven't even opened the dura. The big difference, of course, would be that we've severed every single nerve that leads into it – except for the one optic nerve – and this means that your thinking would no longer be influenced by your senses. You'd be living in an extraordinarily pure and detached world. Nothing to bother you at all, not even pain. You couldn't possibly feel pain because there wouldn't be any nerves to feel it with. In a way, it would be an almost perfect situation. No worries or fears or pains or hunger or thirst. Not even any desires. Just your memories and your *thoughts, and if the remaining eye happened to function, then you could read books as well. It all sounds rather pleasant to me.'*

'It does, does it?'

'Yes, William, it does. And particularly for a Doctor of Philosophy. It would be a tremendous experience. You'd be able to reflect upon the ways of the world with a detachment and a serenity that no man had ever attained before. And who knows what might not happen then! Great thoughts and solutions might come to you, great ideas that could revolutionize our way of life! Try to imagine, if you can, the degree of concentration that you'd be able to achieve!'

'And the frustration,' I said.

'Nonsense. There couldn't be any frustration. You can't have frustration without desire, and you couldn't possibly have any desire. Not physical desire, anyway.'

'I should certainly be capable of remembering my previous life in the world, and I might desire to return to it.'

'What, to this mess! Out of your comfortable basin and back into this madhouse!'

'Answer one more question,' I said. 'How long do you believe you could keep it alive?'

'The brain? Who knows? Possibly for years and years. The conditions would be ideal. Most of the factors that cause deterioration would be absent, thanks to the artificial heart. The blood-pressure would remain constant at all times, an impossible condition in real life. The temperature would also be constant. The chemical composition of the blood would be near perfect. There would be no impurities in it, no virus, no bacteria, nothing. Of course it's foolish to guess, but I believe that a brain might live for two or three hundred years in circumstances like these. Good-bye

for now,' he said. 'I'll drop in and see you tomorrow.' He went out quickly, leaving me, as you might guess, in a fairly disturbed state of mind.

My immediate reaction after he had gone was one of revulsion towards the whole business. Somehow, it wasn't at all nice. There was something basically repulsive about the idea that I myself, with all my mental faculties intact, should be reduced to a small slimy grey blob lying in a pool of water. It was monstrous, obscene, unholy. Another thing that bothered me was the feeling of helplessness that I was bound to experience once Landy had got me into the basin. There could be no going back after that, no way of protesting or explaining. I would be committed for as long as they could keep me alive.

And what, for example, if I could not stand it? What if it turned out to be terribly painful? What if I became hysterical?

No legs to run away on. No voice to scream with. Nothing. I'd just have to grin and bear it for the next two centuries.

No mouth to grin with either.

At this point, a curious thought struck me, and it was this: Does not a man who has had a leg amputated often suffer from the delusion that the leg is still there? Does he not tell the nurse that the toes he doesn't have any more are itching like mad, and so on and so forth? I seemed to have heard something to that effect quite recently.

Very well. On the same premise, was it not possible that my brain, lying there alone in that basin, might not suffer from a similar delusion in regard to my body? In which case, all my usual aches and pains could come flooding over me and I wouldn't even be able to take an aspirin to relieve them. One moment I might be imagining that I had the most excruciating cramp in my leg, or a violent indigestion, and a few minutes later, I might easily get the feeling that my poor bladder — you know me — was so full that if I didn't get to emptying it soon it would burst.

Heaven forbid.

I lay there for a long time thinking these horrid thoughts. Then quite suddenly, round about midday, my mood began to change. I became less concerned with the unpleasant aspect of the affair and found myself able to examine Landy's proposals in a more reasonable light. Was there not, after all, I asked myself, something a bit comforting in the thought that my brain might not necessarily have to die and disappear in a few weeks' time? There was indeed. I am rather proud of my brain. It is a sensitive, lucid and uberous organ. It contains a prodigious store of information, and it is still capable of producing imaginative and original theories. As brains go, it is a damn good one, though I say it myself. Whereas my body, my poor old body, the thing that Landy wants to throw away — well, even you, my dear Mary, will have to agree with me that there is really nothing about that which is worth preserving any more.

I was lying on my back eating a grape. Delicious it was, and there were three little seeds in it which I took out of my mouth and placed on the edge of the plate.

'I'm going to do it,' I said quietly. 'Yes, by God, I'm going to do it. When Landy comes back to see me tomorrow I shall tell him straight out that I'm going to do it.'

It was as quick as that. And from then on, I began to feel very much better. I surprised everyone by gobbling an enormous lunch, and shortly after that you came in to visit me as usual.

But how well I looked, you told me. How bright and well and chirpy. Had anything happened? Was there some good news?

Yes, I said, there was. And then, if you remember, I bade you sit down and make yourself comfortable, and I started out immediately to explain to you as gently as I could what was in the wind.

Alas, you would have none of it. I had hardly begun telling you the barest details when you flew into a fury and said that the thing was revolting, disgusting, horrible, unthinkable, and when I tried to go on, you marched out of the room.

Well, Mary, as you know, I have tried to discuss this subject with you many times since then, but you have consistently refused to give me a hearing. Hence this note, and I can only hope that you will have the good sense to permit yourself to read it. It has taken me a long time to write. Two weeks have gone by since I started to scribble the first sentence, and I'm now a good deal weaker than I was then. I doubt I have the strength to say much more. Certainly I won't say good-bye, because there's a chance, just a tiny chance, that if Landy succeeds in his work I may actually see you again later, that is if you can bring yourself to come and visit me.

I am giving orders that these pages shall not be delivered to you until a week after I am gone. By now, therefore, as you sit reading them, seven days have already elapsed since Landy did the deed. You yourself may even know what the outcome has been. If you don't, if you have purposely kept yourself apart and have refused to have anything to do with it – which I suspect may be the case – please change your mind now and give Landy a call to see how things went with me. That is the least you can do. I have told him that he may expect to hear from you on the seventh day.

Your faithful husband
William

P.S. Be good when I am gone, and always remember that it is harder to be a widow than a wife. Do not drink cocktails. Do not waste money. Do not smoke cigarettes. Do not eat pastry. Do not use lipstick. Do not buy a television apparatus. Keep my rose beds and my rockery well weeded in the summers. And incidentally I suggest that you have the telephone disconnected now that I shall have no further use for it.

W.

Mrs Pearl laid the last page of the manuscript slowly down on the sofa beside her. Her little mouth was pursed up tight and there was a whiteness around her nostrils.

But really! You would think a widow was entitled to a bit of peace after all these years.

The whole thing was just too awful to think about. Beastly and awful. It gave her the shudders.

She reached for her bag and found herself another cigarette. She lit it, inhaling the smoke deeply and blowing it out in clouds all over the room. Through the smoke she could see her lovely television set, brand new, lustrous, huge, crouching defiantly but also a little self-consciously on top of what used to be William's worktable.

What would he say, she wondered, if he could see that now?

She paused, to remember the last time he had caught her smoking a cigarette. That was about a year ago, and she was sitting in the kitchen by the open window having a quick one before he came home from work. She'd had the radio on loud playing dance music and she had turned round to pour herself another cup of coffee and there he was standing in the doorway, huge and grim, staring down at her with those awful eyes, a little black dot of fury blazing in the centre of each.

For four weeks after that, he had paid the housekeeping bills himself and given her no money at all, but of course he wasn't to know that she had over six pounds stashed away in a soap-flake carton in the cupboard under the sink.

'What is it?' she had said to him once during supper. 'Are you worried about me getting lung cancer?'

'I am not,' he had answered.

'Then why can't I smoke?'

'Because I disapprove, that's why.'

He had also disapproved of children, and as a result they had never had any of them either.

Where was he now, this William of hers, the great disapprover?

Landy would be expecting her to call up. Did she *have* to call Landy?

Well, not really, no.

She finished her cigarette, then lit another one immediately from the old stub. She looked at the telephone that was sitting on the worktable beside the television set. William had asked her to call. He had specifically requested that she telephone Landy as soon as she had read the letter. She hesitated, fighting hard now against that old ingrained sense of duty that she didn't quite yet dare to shake off. Then, slowly, she got to her feet and crossed over to the phone on the worktable. She found a number in the book, dialled it, and waited.

'I want to speak to Dr Landy, please.'

'Who is calling?'

'Mrs Pearl. Mrs William Pearl.'

'One moment, please.'

Almost at once, Landy was on the other end of the wire.

'Mrs Pearl?'

'This is Mrs Pearl.'

There was a slight pause.

'I am so glad you called at last, Mrs Pearl. You are quite well, I hope?' The voice was quiet, unemotional, courteous. 'I wonder if you would care to come over here to the hospital? Then we can have a little chat. I expect you are very eager to know how it all came out.'

She didn't answer.

'I can tell you now that everything went pretty smoothly, one way and another. Far better, in fact, than I was entitled to hope. It is not only alive, Mrs Pearl, it is conscious. It recovered consciousness on the second day. Isn't that interesting?'

She waited for him to go on.

'And the eye is seeing. We are sure of that because we get an immediate change in the deflections on the encephalograph when we hold something up in front of it. And now we're giving it the newspaper to read every day.'

'Which newspaper?' Mrs Pearl asked sharply.

'The *Daily Mirror*. The headlines are larger.'

'He hates the *Mirror*. Give him *The Times*.'

There was a pause, then the doctor said, 'Very well, Mrs Pearl. We'll give it *The Times*. We naturally want to do all we can to keep it happy.'

'*Him,*' she said. 'Not *it. Him!*'

'Him,' the doctor said. 'Yes, I beg your pardon. To keep him happy. That's one reason why I suggested you should come along here as soon as possible. I think it would be good for him to see you. You could indicate how delighted you were to be with him again – smile at him and blow him a kiss and all that sort of thing. It's bound to be a comfort to him to know that you are standing by.'

There was a long pause.

'Well,' Mrs Pearl said at last, her voice suddenly very meek and tired. 'I suppose I had better come on over and see how he is.'

'Good. I knew you would. I'll wait here for you. Come straight up to my office on the second floor. Good-bye.'

Half an hour later, Mrs Pearl was at the hospital.

'You mustn't be surprised by what he looks like,' Landy said as he walked beside her down a corridor.

'No, I won't.'

'It's bound to be a bit of a shock to you at first. He's not very prepossessing in his present state, I'm afraid.'

'I didn't marry him for his looks, Doctor.'

Landy turned and stared at her. What a queer little woman this was, he thought, with her large eyes and her sullen, resentful air. Her features, which must have been quite pleasant once, had now gone completely. The mouth was slack, the cheeks loose and flabby, and the whole face gave the impression of having slowly but surely sagged to pieces through years and years of joyless married life. They walked on for a while in silence.

'Take your time when you get inside,' Landy said. 'He

won't know you're in there until you place your face directly above his eye. The eye is always open, but he can't move it at all, so the field of vision is very narrow. At present we have it looking straight up at the ceiling. And of course he can't hear anything. We can talk together as much as we like. It's in here.'

Landy opened a door and ushered her into a small square room.

'I wouldn't go too close yet,' he said, putting a hand on her arm. 'Stay back here a moment with me until you get used to it all.'

There was a biggish white enamel bowl about the size of a wash-basin standing on a high white table in the centre of the room, and there were half a dozen thin plastic tubes coming out of it. These tubes were connected with a whole lot of glass piping in which you could see the blood flowing to and from the heart machine. The machine itself made a soft rhythmic pulsing sound.

'He's in there,' Landy said, pointing to the basin, which was too high for her to see into. 'Come just a little closer. Not too near.'

He led her two paces forward.

By stretching her neck, Mrs Pearl could now see the surface of the liquid inside the basin. It was clear and still, and on it there floated a small oval capsule, about the size of a pigeon's egg.

'That's the eye in there,' Landy said. 'Can you see it?'
'Yes.'

'So far as we can tell, it is still in perfect condition. It's his right eye, and the plastic container has a lens on it similar to the one he used in his own spectacles. At this moment he's probably seeing quite as well as he did before.'

'The ceiling isn't much to look at,' Mrs Pearl said.

'Don't worry about that. We're in the process of working out a whole programme to keep him amused, but we don't want to go too quickly at first.'

'Give him a good book.'

'We will, we will. Are you feeling all right, Mrs Pearl?'

'Yes.'

'Then we'll go forward a little more, shall we, and you'll be able to see the whole thing.'

He led her forward until they were standing only a couple of yards from the table, and now she could see right down into the basin.

'There you are,' Landy said. 'That's William.'

He was far larger than she had imagined he would be, and darker in colour. With all the ridges and creases running over his surface, he reminded her of nothing so much as an enormous pickled walnut. She could see the stubs of the four big arteries and the two veins coming out from the base of him and the neat way in which they were joined to the plastic tubes; and with each throb of the heart machine, all the tubes gave a little jerk in unison as the blood was pushed through them.

'You'll have to lean over,' Landy said, 'and put your pretty face right above the eye. He'll see you then, and you can smile at him and blow him a kiss. If I were you I'd say a few nice things as well. He won't actually hear them, but I'm sure he'll get the general idea.'

'He hates people blowing kisses at him,' Mrs Pearl said.

'I'll do it my own way if you don't mind.' She stepped up to the edge of the table, leaned forward until her face was directly over the basin, and looked straight down into William's eye.

'Hallo, dear,' she whispered. 'It's me – Mary.'

The eye, bright as ever, stared back at her with a peculiar, fixed intensity.

'How are you, dear?' she said.

The plastic capsule was transparent all the way round so that the whole of the eyeball was visible. The optic nerve connecting the underside of it to the brain looked like a short length of grey spaghetti.

'Are you feeling all right, William?'

It was a queer sensation peering into her husband's eye when there was no face to go with it. All she had to look at was the eye, and she kept staring at it, and gradually it grew bigger and bigger, and in the end it was the only thing that she could see – a sort of face in itself. There was a network of tiny red veins running over the white surface of the eyeball, and in the ice-blue of the iris there were three or four rather pretty darkish streaks radiating from the pupil in the centre. The pupil was large and black, with a little spark of light reflecting from one side of it.

'I got your letter, dear, and came over at once to see how you were. Dr Landy says you are doing wonderfully well. Perhaps if I talk slowly you can understand a little of what I am saying by reading my lips.'

There was no doubt that the eye was watching her.

'They are doing everything possible to take care of you,

dear. This marvellous machine thing here is pumping away all the time and I'm sure it's a lot better than those silly old hearts all the rest of us have. Ours are liable to break down any moment, but yours will go on for ever.'

She was studying the eye closely, trying to discover what there was about it that gave it such an unusual appearance.

'You seem fine, dear, just fine. Really you do.'

It looked ever so much nicer, this eye, than either of his eyes used to look, she told herself. There was a softness about it somewhere, a calm, kindly quality that she had never seen before. Maybe it had to do with the dot in the very centre, the pupil. William's pupils used always to be tiny black pinheads. They used to glint at you, stabbing into your brain, seeing right through you, and they always knew at once what you were up to and even what you were thinking. But this one she was looking at now was large and soft and gentle, almost cowlike.

'Are you quite sure he's conscious?' she asked, not looking up.

'Oh yes, completely,' Landy said.

'And he *can* see me?'

'Perfectly.'

'Isn't that marvellous? I expect he's wondering what happened.'

'Not at all. He knows perfectly well where he is and why he's there. He can't possibly have forgotten that.'

'You mean he *knows* he's in this basin?'

'Of course. And if only he had the power of speech, he would probably be able to carry on a perfectly normal conversation with you this very minute. So far as I can see, there should be absolutely no difference mentally between this William here and the one you used to know back home.'

'Good *gracious* me,' Mrs Pearl said, and she paused to consider this intriguing aspect.

You know what, she told herself, looking behind the eye now and staring hard at the great grey pulpy walnut that lay so placidly under the water. I'm not at all sure that I don't prefer him as he is at present. In fact, I believe that I could live very comfortably with this kind of a William. I could cope with this one.

'Quiet, isn't he?' she said.

'Naturally he's quiet.'

No arguments and criticisms, she thought, no constant admonitions, no rules to obey, no ban on smoking cigarettes, no pair of cold disapproving eyes watching me over the top of a book in the evenings, no shirts to wash and iron, no meals to cook – nothing but the throb of the heart machine, which was rather a soothing sound anyway and certainly not loud enough to interfere with television.

'Doctor,' she said. 'I do believe I'm suddenly getting to feel the most enormous affection for him. Does that sound queer?'

'I think it's quite understandable.'

'He looks so helpless and silent lying there under the water in his little basin.'

'Yes, I know.'

'He's like a baby, that's what he's like. He's exactly like a little baby.'

Landy stood still behind her, watching.

'There,' she said softly, peering into the basin. 'From now on Mary's going to look after you *all* by herself and you've nothing to worry about in the world. When can I have him back home, Doctor?'

'I beg your pardon?'

'I said when can I have him back – back in my own house?'

'You're joking,' Landy said.

She turned her head slowly round and looked directly at him. 'Why should I joke?' she asked. Her face was bright, her eyes round and bright as two diamonds.

'He couldn't possibly be moved.'

'I don't see why not.'

'This is an experiment, Mrs Pearl.'

'It's my husband, Dr Landy.'

A funny little nervous half-smile appeared on Landy's mouth. 'Well . . .' he said.

'It *is* my husband, you know.' There was no anger in her voice. She spoke quietly, as though merely reminding him of a simple fact.

'That's rather a tricky point,' Landy said, wetting his lips. 'You're a widow now, Mrs Pearl. I think you must resign yourself to that fact.'

She turned away suddenly from the table and crossed over to the window. 'I mean it,' she said, fishing in her bag for a cigarette. 'I want him back.'

Landy watched her as she put the cigarette between her lips and lit it. Unless he were very much mistaken, there was something a bit odd about this woman, he thought.

She seemed almost pleased to have her husband over there in the basin.

He tried to imagine what his own feelings would be if it were *his* wife's brain lying there and *her* eye staring up at him out of that capsule.

He wouldn't like it.

'Shall we go back to my room now?' he said.

She was standing by the window, apparently quite calm and relaxed, puffing her cigarette.

'Yes, all right.'

On her way past the table she stopped and leaned over the basin once more. 'Mary's leaving now, sweetheart,' she said. 'And don't you worry about a single thing, you understand? We're going to get you right back home where we can look after you properly just as soon as we possibly can. And listen, dear . . .' At this point she paused and carried the cigarette to her lips, intending to take a puff.

Instantly the eye flashed.

She was looking straight into it at the time, and right in the centre of it she saw a tiny but brilliant flash of light, and the pupil contracted into a minute black pinpoint of absolute fury.

At first she didn't move. She stood bending over the basin, holding the cigarette up to her mouth, watching the eye.

Then very slowly, deliberately, she put the cigarette between her lips and took a long suck. She inhaled deeply, and she held the smoke inside her lungs for three or four seconds; then suddenly, *whoosh*, out it came through her nostrils in two thin jets which struck the water in the basin and billowed out over the surface in a thick blue cloud, enveloping the eye.

Landy was over by the door, with his back to her, waiting. 'Come on, Mrs Pearl,' he called.

'Don't look so cross, William,' she said softly. 'It isn't any good looking cross.'

Landy turned his head to see what she was doing.

'Not any more it isn't,' she whispered. 'Because from now on, my pet, you're going to do just exactly what Mary tells you. Do you understand that?'

'Mrs Pearl,' Landy said, moving towards her.

'So don't be a naughty boy again, will you, my precious,' she said, taking another pull at the cigarette. 'Naughty boys are liable to get punished most severely nowadays, you ought to know that.'

Landy was beside her now, and he took her by the arm and began drawing her firmly but gently away from the table.

'Good-bye, darling,' she called. 'I'll be back soon.'

'That's enough, Mrs Pearl.'

'Isn't he sweet?' she cried, looking up at Landy with big bright eyes. 'Isn't he darling? I just can't wait to get him home.'

The Way Up to Heaven

First published in the *New Yorker*,
27 February 1954

All her life, Mrs Foster had had an almost pathological fear of missing a train, a plane, a boat or even a theatre curtain. In other respects, she was not a particularly nervous woman, but the mere thought of being late on occasions like these would throw her into such a state of nerves that she would begin to twitch. It was nothing much – just a tiny vellicating muscle in the corner of the left eye, like a secret wink – but the annoying thing was that it refused to disappear until an hour or so after the train or plane or whatever it was had been safely caught.

It is really extraordinary how in certain people a simple apprehension about a thing like catching a train can grow into a serious obsession. At least half an hour before it was time to leave the house for the station, Mrs Foster would step out of the elevator all ready to go, with hat and coat and gloves, and then, being quite unable to sit down, she would flutter and fidget about from room to room until her husband, who must have been well aware of her state, finally emerged from his privacy and suggested in a cool dry voice that perhaps they had better get going now, had they not?

Mr Foster may possibly have had a right to be irritated by this foolishness of his wife's, but he could have had no excuse for increasing her misery by keeping her waiting unnecessarily. Mind you, it is by no means certain that this is what he did, yet whenever they were to go somewhere, his timing was so accurate – just a minute or two late, you understand – and his manner so bland that it was hard to believe he wasn't purposely inflicting a nasty private little torture of his own on the unhappy lady. And one thing he must have known – that she would never dare to call out and tell him to hurry. He had disciplined her too well for that. He must also have known that if he was prepared to wait even beyond the last moment of safety, he could drive her nearly into hysterics. On one or two special occasions in the later years of their married life, it seemed almost as though he had *wanted* to miss the train simply in order to intensify the poor woman's suffering.

Assuming (though one cannot be sure) that the husband was guilty, what made his attitude doubly unreasonable was the fact that, with the exception of this one small irrepressible foible, Mrs Foster was and always had been a good and loving wife. For over thirty years, she had served him loyally and well. There was no doubt about this. Even she, a very modest woman, was aware of it, and although she had for years refused to let herself believe that Mr Foster would ever consciously torment her, there had been times recently when she had caught herself beginning to wonder.

Mr Eugene Foster, who was nearly seventy years old, lived with his wife in a large six-storey house on East Sixty-second Street, and they had four servants. It was a gloomy place, and few people came to visit them. But on this particular morning in January, the house had come alive and there was a great deal of bustling about. One maid was distributing bundles of dust sheets to every room, while another was draping them over the furniture. The butler was bringing down suitcases and putting them in the hall. The cook kept popping up from the kitchen to have a word with the butler, and Mrs Foster herself, in an old-fashioned fur coat and with a black hat on the top of her head, was flying from room to room and pretending to supervise these operations. Actually, she was thinking of nothing at all except that she was going to miss her plane if her husband didn't come out of his study soon and get ready.

'What time is it, Walker?' she said to the butler as she passed him.

'It's ten minutes past nine, Madam.'

'And has the car come?'

'Yes, Madam, it's waiting. I'm just going to put the luggage in now.'

'It takes an hour to get to Idlewild,' she said. 'My plane leaves at eleven. I have to be there half an hour beforehand for the formalities. I shall be late. I just *know* I'm going to be late.'

'I think you have plenty of time, Madam,' the butler said kindly. 'I warned Mr Foster that you must leave at nine fifteen. There's still another five minutes.'

'Yes, Walker, I know, I know. But get the luggage in quickly, will you please?'

She began walking up and down the hall, and whenever the butler came by, she asked him the time. This, she kept telling herself, was the *one* plane she must not miss. It had taken her months to persuade her husband to allow her to go. If she missed it, he might easily decide that she should cancel the whole thing. And the trouble was that he insisted on coming to the airport to see her off.

'Dear God,' she said aloud, 'I'm going to miss it. I know, I know, I *know* I'm going to miss it.' The little muscle beside the left eye was twitching madly now. The eyes themselves were very close to tears.

'What time is it, Walker?'

'It's eighteen minutes past, Madam.'

'Now I really *will* miss it!' she cried. 'Oh, I wish he would come!'

This was an important journey for Mrs Foster. She was going all alone to Paris to visit her daughter, her only child, who was married to a Frenchman. Mrs Foster didn't care much for the Frenchman, but she was fond of her daughter, and, more than that, she had developed a great yearning to set eyes on her three grandchildren. She knew them only from the many photographs that she had received and that she kept putting up all over the house. They were beautiful, these children. She doted on them, and each time a new picture arrived, she would carry it away and sit with it for a long time, staring at it lovingly and searching the small faces for signs of that old satisfying blood likeness that meant so much. And now, lately, she had come more and more to feel that she did not really wish to live out her days in a place where she could not be near these children, and have them visit her, and take them for walks, and buy them presents, and watch them grow. She knew, of course, that it was wrong and in a way disloyal to have thoughts like these while her husband was still alive. She knew also that although he was no longer active in his many enterprises, he would never consent to leave New York and live in Paris. It was a miracle that he had ever agreed to let her fly over there alone for six weeks to visit them. But, oh, how she wished she could live there always, and be close to them!

'Walker, what time is it?'

'Twenty-two minutes past, Madam.'

As he spoke, a door opened and Mr Foster came into the hall. He stood for a moment, looking intently at his wife, and she looked back at him – at this diminutive but still quite dapper old man with the huge bearded face that bore such an astonishing resemblance to those old photographs of Andrew Carnegie.

'Well,' he said, 'I suppose perhaps we'd better get going fairly soon if you want to catch that plane.'

'*Yes*, dear – *yes*! Everything's ready. The car's waiting.'

'That's good,' he said. With his head over to one side, he was watching her closely. He had a peculiar way of cocking the head and then moving it in a series of small, rapid jerks. Because of this and because he was clasping his hands up high in front of him, near the chest, he was somehow like a squirrel standing there – a quick clever old squirrel from the Park.

'Here's Walker with your coat, dear. Put it on.'

'I'll be with you in a moment,' he said. 'I'm just going to wash my hands.'

She waited for him, and the tall butler stood beside her, holding the coat and the hat.

'Walker, will I miss it?'

'No, Madam,' the butler said. 'I think you'll make it all right.'

Then Mr Foster appeared again, and the butler helped him on with his coat. Mrs Foster hurried outside and got into the hired Cadillac. Her husband came after her, but he walked down the steps of the house slowly, pausing half-way to observe the sky and to sniff the cold morning air.

'It looks a bit foggy,' he said as he sat down beside her in the car. 'And it's always worse out there at the airport. I shouldn't be surprised if the flight's cancelled already.'

'Don't say that, dear – *please*.'

They didn't speak again until the car had crossed over the river to Long Island.

'I arranged everything with the servants,' Mr Foster said. 'They're all going off today. I gave them half pay for six weeks and told Walker I'd send him a telegram when we wanted them back.'

'Yes,' she said. 'He told me.'

'I'll move into the club tonight. It'll be a nice change staying at the club.'

'Yes, dear. I'll write to you.'

'I'll call in at the house occasionally to see that everything's all right and to pick up the mail.'

'But don't you really think Walker should stay there all the time to look after things?' she asked meekly.

'Nonsense. It's quite unnecessary. And anyway, I'd have to pay him full wages.'

'Oh yes,' she said. 'Of course.'

'What's more, you never know what people get up to

when they're left alone in a house,' Mr Foster announced, and with that he took out a cigar and, after snipping off the end with a silver cutter, lit it with a gold lighter.

She sat still in the car with her hands clasped together tight under the rug.

'Will you write to me?' she asked.

'I'll see,' he said. 'But I doubt it. You know I don't hold with letter-writing unless there's something specific to say.'

'Yes, dear, I know. So don't you bother.'

They drove on, along Queens Boulevard, and as they approached the flat marshland on which Idlewild is built, the fog began to thicken and the car had to slow down.

'Oh dear!' cried Mrs Foster. 'I'm *sure* I'm going to miss it now! What time is it?'

'Stop fussing,' the old man said. 'It doesn't matter anyway. It's bound to be cancelled now. They never fly in this sort of weather. I don't know why you bothered to come out.'

She couldn't be sure, but it seemed to her that there was suddenly a new note in his voice, and she turned to look at him. It was difficult to observe any change in his expression under all that hair. The mouth was what counted. She wished, as she had so often before, that she could see the mouth clearly. The eyes never showed anything except when he was in a rage.

'Of course,' he went on, 'if by any chance it *does* go, then I agree with you – you'll be certain to miss it now. Why don't you resign yourself to that?'

She turned away and peered through the window at the fog. It seemed to be getting thicker as they went along, and now she could only just make out the edge of the road and the margin of grassland beyond it. She knew that her husband was still looking at her. She glanced back at him again, and this time she noticed with a kind of horror that he was staring intently at the little place in the corner of her left eye where she could feel the muscle twitching.

'Won't you?' he said.

'Won't I what?'

'Be sure to miss it now if it goes. We can't drive fast in this muck.'

He didn't speak to her any more after that. The car crawled on and on. The driver had a yellow lamp directed on to the edge of the road and this helped him to keep going. Other lights, some white and some yellow, kept coming out of the fog towards them, and there was an especially bright one that followed close behind them all the time.

Suddenly, the driver stopped the car.

'There!' Mr Foster cried. 'We're stuck. I knew it.'

'No, sir,' the driver said, turning round. 'We made it. This is the airport.'

Without a word, Mrs Foster jumped out and hurried through the main entrance into the building. There was a mass of people inside, mostly disconsolate passengers standing around the ticket counters. She pushed her way through and spoke to the clerk.

'Yes,' he said. 'Your flight is temporarily postponed.

But please don't go away. We're expecting this weather to clear any moment.'

She went back to her husband who was still sitting in the car and told him the news. 'But don't you wait, dear,' she said. 'There's no sense in that.'

'I won't,' he answered. 'So long as the driver can get me back. Can you get me back, driver?'

'I think so,' the man said.

'Is the luggage out?'

'Yes, sir.'

'Good-bye, dear,' Mrs Foster said, leaning into the car and giving her husband a small kiss on the coarse grey fur of his cheek.

'Good-bye,' he answered. 'Have a good trip.'

The car drove off, and Mrs Foster was left alone.

The rest of the day was a sort of nightmare for her. She sat for hour after hour on a bench, as close to the airline counter as possible, and every thirty minutes or so she would get up and ask the clerk if the situation had changed. She always received the same reply – that she must continue to wait, because the fog might blow away at any moment. It wasn't until after six in the evening that the loudspeakers finally announced that the flight had been postponed until eleven o'clock the next morning.

Mrs Foster didn't quite know what to do when she heard this news. She stayed sitting on her bench for at least another half-hour, wondering, in a tired, hazy sort of way, where she might go to spend the night. She hated to leave the airport. She didn't wish to see her husband. She was terrified that in one way or another he would eventually manage to prevent her from getting to France. She would have liked to remain just where she was, sitting on the bench the whole night through. That would be the safest. But she was already exhausted, and it didn't take her long to realize that this was a ridiculous thing for an elderly lady to do. So in the end she went to a phone and called the house.

Her husband, who was on the point of leaving for the club, answered it himself. She told him the news, and asked whether the servants were still there.

'They've all gone,' he said.

'In that case, dear, I'll just get myself a room somewhere for the night. And don't you bother yourself about it at all.'

'That would be foolish,' he said. 'You've got a large house here at your disposal. Use it.'

'But, dear, it's *empty*.'

'Then I'll stay with you myself.'

'There's no food in the house. There's nothing.'

'Then eat before you come in. Don't be so stupid, woman. Everything you do, you seem to want to make a fuss about it.'

'Yes,' she said. 'I'm sorry. I'll get myself a sandwich here, and then I'll come on in.'

Outside, the fog had cleared a little, but it was still a long, slow drive in the taxi, and she didn't arrive back at the house on Sixty-second Street until fairly late.

Her husband emerged from his study when he heard her coming in. 'Well,' he said, standing by the study door, 'how was Paris?'

'We leave at eleven in the morning,' she answered. 'It's definite.'

'You mean if the fog clears.'

'It's clearing now. There's a wind coming up.'

'You look tired,' he said. 'You must have had an anxious day.'

'It wasn't very comfortable. I think I'll go straight to bed.'

'I've ordered a car for the morning,' he said. 'Nine o'clock.'

'Oh, thank you, dear. And I certainly hope you're not going to bother to come all the way out again to see me off.'

'No,' he said slowly. 'I don't think I will. But there's no reason why you shouldn't drop me at the club on your way.'

She looked at him, and at that moment he seemed to be standing a long way off from her, beyond some border-line. He was suddenly so small and far away that she couldn't be sure what he was doing, or what he was thinking, or even what he was.

'The club is downtown,' she said. 'It isn't on the way to the airport.'

'But you'll have plenty of time, my dear. Don't you want to drop me at the club?'

'Oh, yes – of course.'

'That's good. Then I'll see you in the morning at nine.'

She went up to her bedroom on the third floor, and she was so exhausted from her day that she fell asleep soon after she lay down.

Next morning, Mrs Foster was up early, and by eight thirty she was downstairs and ready to leave.

Shortly after nine, her husband appeared. 'Did you make any coffee?' he asked.

'No, dear. I thought you'd get a nice breakfast at the club. The car is here. It's been waiting. I'm all ready to go.'

They were standing in the hall – they always seemed to be meeting in the hall nowadays – she with her hat and coat and purse, he in a curiously cut Edwardian jacket with high lapels.

'Your luggage?'

'It's at the airport.'

'Ah yes,' he said. 'Of course. And if you're going to take me to the club first, I suppose we'd better get going fairly soon, hadn't we?'

'Yes!' she cried. 'Oh, yes – *please*!'

'I'm just going to get a few cigars. I'll be right with you. You get in the car.'

She turned and went out to where the chauffeur was standing, and he opened the car door for her as she approached.

'What time is it?' she asked him.

'About nine fifteen.'

Mr Foster came out five minutes later, and watching him as he walked slowly down the steps, she noticed that his legs were like goat's legs in those narrow stovepipe trousers that he wore. As on the day before, he paused halfway down to sniff the air and to examine the sky. The weather was still not quite clear, but there was a wisp of sun coming through the mist.

'Perhaps you'll be lucky this time,' he said as he settled himself beside her in the car.

'Hurry, please,' she said to the chauffeur. 'Don't bother about the rug. I'll arrange the rug. Please get going. I'm late.'

The man went back to his seat behind the wheel and started the engine.

'*Just* a moment!' Mr Foster said suddenly. 'Hold it a moment, chauffeur, will you?'

'What is it, dear?' She saw him searching the pockets of his overcoat.

'I had a little present I wanted you to take to Ellen,' he said. 'Now, where on earth is it? I'm sure I had it in my hand as I came down.'

'I never saw you carrying anything. What sort of present?'

'A little box wrapped up in white paper. I forgot to give it to you yesterday. I don't want to forget it today.'

'A little box!' Mrs Foster cried. 'I never saw any little box!' She began hunting frantically in the back of the car.

Her husband continued searching through the pockets of his coat. Then he unbuttoned the coat and felt around in his jacket. 'Confound it,' he said, 'I must've left it in my bedroom. I won't be a moment.'

'Oh, *please*!' she cried. 'We haven't got time! *Please* leave it! You can mail it. It's only one of those silly combs anyway. You're always giving her combs.'

'And what's wrong with combs, may I ask?' he said, furious that she should have forgotten herself for once.

'Nothing, dear, I'm sure. But . . .'

231

'Stay here!' he commanded. 'I'm going to get it.'

'Be quick, dear! Oh, *please* be quick!'

She sat still, waiting and waiting.

'Chauffeur, what time is it?'

The man had a wristwatch, which he consulted. 'I make it nearly nine thirty.'

'Can we get to the airport in an hour?'

'Just about.'

At this point, Mrs Foster suddenly spotted a corner of something white wedged down in the crack of the seat on the side where her husband had been sitting. She reached over and pulled out a small paper-wrapped box, and at the same time she couldn't help noticing that it was wedged down firm and deep, as though with the help of a pushing hand.

'Here it is!' she cried. 'I've found it! Oh dear, and now he'll be up there forever searching for it! Chauffeur, quickly – run in and call him down, will you please?'

The chauffeur, a man with a small rebellious Irish mouth, didn't care very much for any of this, but he climbed out of the car and went up the steps to the front door of the house. Then he turned and came back. 'Door's locked,' he announced. 'You got a key?'

'Yes – wait a minute.' She began hunting madly in her purse. The little face was screwed up tight with anxiety, the lips pushed outwards like a sprout.

'Here it is! No – I'll go myself. It'll be quicker. I know where he'll be.'

She hurried out of the car and up the steps to the front

door, holding the key in one hand. She slid the key into the keyhole and was about to turn it – and then she stopped. Her head came up, and she stood there absolutely motionless, her whole body arrested right in the middle of all this hurry to turn the key and get into the house, and she waited – five, six, seven, eight, nine, ten seconds, she waited. The way she was standing there, with her head in the air and the body so tense, it seemed as though she were listening for the repetition of some sound that she had heard a moment before from a place far away inside the house.

Yes – quite obviously she was listening. Her whole attitude was a *listening* one. She appeared actually to be moving one of her ears closer and closer to the door. Now it was right up against the door, and for still another few seconds she remained in that position, head up, ear to door, hand on key, about to enter but not entering, trying instead, or so it seemed, to hear and to analyse these sounds that were coming faintly from this place deep within the house.

Then, all at once, she sprang to life again. She withdrew the key from the door and came running back down the steps.

'It's too late!' she cried to the chauffeur. 'I can't wait for him, I simply can't. I'll miss the plane. Hurry now, driver, hurry! To the airport!'

The chauffeur, had he been watching her closely, might have noticed that her face had turned absolutely white and that the whole expression had suddenly altered. There was no longer that rather soft and silly look. A peculiar hardness had settled itself upon the features. The little mouth, usually so flabby, was now tight and thin, the eyes were bright, and the voice, when she spoke, carried a new note of authority.

'Hurry, driver, hurry!'

'Isn't your husband travelling with you?' the man asked, astonished.

'Certainly not! I was only going to drop him at the club. It won't matter. He'll understand. He'll get a cab. Don't sit there talking, man. *Get going!* I've got a plane to catch for Paris!'

With Mrs Foster urging him from the back seat, the man drove fast all the way, and she caught her plane with a few minutes to spare. Soon she was high up over the Atlantic, reclining comfortably in her aeroplane chair, listening to the hum of the motors, heading for Paris at last. The new mood was still with her. She felt remarkably strong and, in a queer sort of way, wonderful. She was a trifle breathless with it all, but this was more from pure astonishment at what she had done than anything else, and as the plane flew farther and farther away from New York and East Sixty-second Street, a great sense of calmness began to settle upon her. By the time she reached Paris, she was just as strong and cool and calm as she could wish.

She met her grandchildren, and they were even more beautiful in the flesh than in their photographs. They were like angels, she told herself, so beautiful they were. And every day she took them for walks, and fed them cakes, and bought them presents, and told them charming stories.

Once a week, on Tuesdays, she wrote a letter to her husband – a nice, chatty letter – full of news and gossip, which always ended with the words 'Now be sure to take your meals regularly, dear, although this is something I'm afraid you may not be doing when I'm not with you.'

When the six weeks were up, everybody was sad that she had to return to America, to her husband. Everybody, that is, except her. Surprisingly, she didn't seem to mind as much as one might have expected, and when she kissed them all good-bye, there was something in her manner and in the things she said that appeared to hint at the possibility of a return in the not too distant future.

However, like the faithful wife she was, she did not overstay her time. Exactly six weeks after she had arrived, she sent a cable to her husband and caught the plane back to New York.

Arriving at Idlewild, Mrs Foster was interested to observe that there was no car to meet her. It is possible that she might even have been a little amused. But she was extremely calm and did not overtip the porter who helped her into a taxi with her baggage.

New York was colder than Paris, and there were lumps of dirty snow lying in the gutters of the streets. The taxi drew up before the house on Sixty-second Street, and Mrs Foster persuaded the driver to carry her two large cases to the top of the steps. Then she paid him off and rang the bell. She waited, but there was no answer. Just to make sure, she rang again, and she could hear it tinkling shrilly far away in the pantry, at the back of the house. But still no one came.

So she took out her own key and opened the door herself.

The first thing she saw as she entered was a great pile of mail lying on the floor where it had fallen after being slipped through the letterbox. The place was dark and cold. A dust sheet was still draped over the grandfather clock. In spite of the cold, the atmosphere was peculiarly oppressive, and there was a faint but curious odour in the air that she had never smelled before.

She walked quickly across the hall and disappeared for a moment round the corner to the left, at the back. There was something deliberate and purposeful about this action; she had the air of a woman who is off to investigate a rumour or to confirm a suspicion. And when she returned a few seconds later, there was a little glimmer of satisfaction on her face.

She paused in the centre of the hall, as though wondering what to do next. Then suddenly, she turned and went across into her husband's study. On the desk she found his address book, and after hunting through it for a while she picked up the phone and dialled a number.

'Hello,' she said. 'Listen – this is Nine East Sixty-second Street . . . Yes, that's right. Could you send someone round as soon as possible, do you think? Yes, it seems to be stuck between the second and third floors. At least, that's where the indicator's pointing . . . Right away? Oh, that's very kind of you. You see, my legs aren't any too good for walking up a lot of stairs. Thank you so much. Good-bye.'

She replaced the receiver and sat there at her husband's desk, patiently waiting for the man who would be coming soon to repair the elevator.

ROALD DAHL

Roald Dahl was a spy, ace fighter-pilot, chocolate historian and medical inventor. He was also the author of Charlie and the Chocolate Factory, Matilda, The BFG and many more brilliant stories. He remains the World's No.1 storyteller.

CHARMING BAKER

Born in Hampshire 1964, Charming Baker spent much of his early life travelling around the world following his father, a commando in the British Army. At the age of twelve, he and his family finally settled in Ripon, North Yorkshire. Baker left school at sixteen and worked various manual jobs. In 1985, having gone back to college, he was accepted onto a course at the prestigious Central Saint Martin's, where he later returned as a lecturer. After graduating, Baker worked for many years as a commercial artist as well as developing his personal work.

Solo exhibitions include the Truman Brewery, London, 2007, Redchurch Street Gallery, London, 2009, New York Studio Gallery, NYC, 2010, Mercer Street, London, 2011 and Milk Studios, LA, 2013. Baker has also exhibited with the Fine Art Society, collaborated with Sir Paul Smith for a sculpture entitled 'Triumph in the Face of Absurdity', which was displayed at the Victoria and Albert Museum, and continues to be committed to creating work to raise money for many charities. He has recently been commissioned to be a presenter on *The Art Show*. His work is in many international collections.

Although Baker has produced sculptural pieces in a wide and varied choice of materials, as well as many large-scale and detailed drawings, he remains primarily a painter with an interest in narrative and an understanding of the tradition of painting. Known to purposefully damage his work by drilling, cutting and even shooting it, Baker intentionally puts in to question the preciousness of art and the definition of its beauty, adding to the emotive charge of the work he produces. Indeed Edward Lucie-Smith has described Baker's paintings as having, something more, a kind of romantic melancholy that is very British. And sometimes the melancholy turns out to have sharp claws. The pictures make you sit up and examine your conscience.

Charming Baker lives and works in London.

CRUELTY
Tales of Malice and Greed

Even when we mean to be kind we can sometimes be cruel. We each have a streak of nastiness inside us. In these ten tales of cruelty Roald Dahl explores how and why it is we make others suffer.

Among others, you'll read the story of two young bullies and the boy they torment, the adulterous wife who uncovers her husband's secret, the man with a painting tattooed on his back whose value he doesn't appreciate and the butler and chef who run rings around their obnoxious employer.

DECEPTION
Tales of Intrigue and Lies

Why do we lie? Why do we deceive those we love most? What do we fear revealing? In these ten tales of deception Roald Dahl explores our tireless efforts to hide the truth about ourselves.

Here, among many others tales you'll read about how to get away with the perfect murder, the old man whose wagers end in a most disturbing payment, how revenge is sweeter when it is carried out by someone else and the card sharp so good at cheating he does something surprising with his life.

LUST
Tales of Craving and Desire

To what lengths would you go to achieve your heart's desire? In these ten tales of maddening lust Roald Dahl explores how our darkest impulses reveal who we really are.

Here you will read a story concerning wife swapping with a twist, hear of the aphrodisiac that drives men into a frenzy, discover the last act in a tale of jilted first love and discover the naked truth of art.

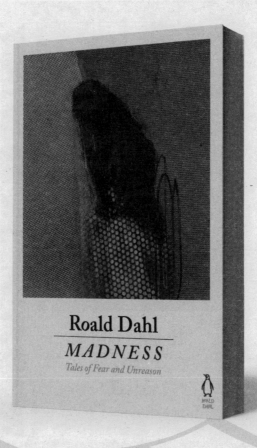

MADNESS
Tales of Fear and Unreason

Our greatest fear is of losing control – above all, of losing control of ourselves. In these ten unsettling tales of unexpected madness Roald Dahl explores what happens when we let go of our sanity.

Among other stories, you'll meet the husband with a jealous fixation on the family cat, the landlady who wants her guests to stay forever, the man whose taste for pork leads him astray and the wife with a pathological fear of being late.

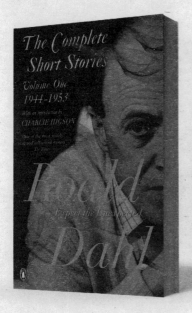

THE COMPLETE ROALD DAHL
SHORT STORIES VOL 1 & 2

*'They are brutal, these stories, and yet you finish
reading each one with a smile, or maybe even a
hollow laugh, certainly a shiver of gratification,
because the conclusion always seems so right'*
Charlie Higson

In these two volumes chronologically collecting all Roald Dahl's 55
published adult short stories, written between 1944 and 1988, and
introduced by Charlie Higson and Anthony Horowitz, we see Roald
Dahl's powerful and dark imagination pen some of the most unsettling
and disquieting tales ever written.

Whether you're young or old, once you've stepped into the brilliant,
troubling world of Roald Dahl, you'll never be the same again.

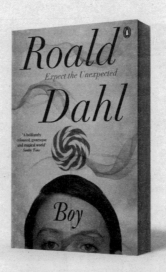

BOY

'An autobiography is a book a person writes about his own life and it is usually full of all sorts of boring details. This is not an autobiography. I would never write a history of myself. On the other hand, throughout my young days at school and just afterwards a number of things happened to me that I have never forgotten . . .'

Boy is a funny, insightful and at times grotesque glimpse into the early life of Roald Dahl. We discover his experiences of the English public school system, the idyllic paradise of summer holidays in Norway, the pleasures (and pains) of the sweetshop, and how it is that he avoided being a Boazer.

This is the unadulterated childhood – sad and funny, macabre and delightful – which speaks of an age which vanished with the coming of the Second World War.

'A shimmering fabric of his yesterdays, the magic and the hurt' *Observer*

'As frightening and funny as his fiction' *The New York Times Book Review*

'Superbly written. A glimpse of a brilliant eccentric' *New Statesman*

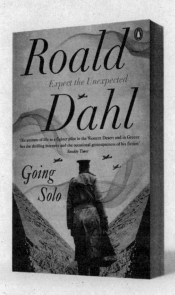

GOING SOLO

'They did not think for one moment that they would find anything but a burnt-out fuselage and a charred skeleton, and they were astounded when they came upon my still-breathing body lying in the sand nearby.'

In 1938 Roald Dahl was fresh out of school and bound for his first job in Africa, hoping to find adventure far from home. However, he got far more excitement than he bargained for when the outbreak of the Second World War led him to join the RAF. His account of his experiences in Africa, crashing a plane in the Western Desert, rescue and recovery from his horrific injuries in Alexandria, flying a Hurricane as Greece fell to the Germans, and many other daring deeds, recreates a world as bizarre and unnerving as any he wrote about in his fiction.

'Very nearly as grotesque as his fiction. The same compulsive blend of wide-eyed innocence and fascination with danger and horror' *Evening Standard*

'A non-stop demonstration of expert raconteurship'
The New York Times Book Review

He just wanted a decent book to read ...

Not too much to ask, is it? It was in 1935 when Allen Lane, Managing Director of Bodley Head Publishers, stood on a platform at Exeter railway station looking for something good to read on his journey back to London. His choice was limited to popular magazines and poor-quality paperbacks – the same choice faced every day by the vast majority of readers, few of whom could afford hardbacks. Lane's disappointment and subsequent anger at the range of books generally available led him to found a company – and change the world.

'We believed in the existence in this country of a vast reading public for intelligent books at a low price, and staked everything on it.'
Sir Allen Lane, 1902–1970, founder of Penguin Books

The quality paperback had arrived – and not just in bookshops. Lane was adamant that his Penguins should appear in chain stores and tobacconists, and should cost no more than a packet of cigarettes.

Reading habits (and cigarette prices) have changed since 1935, but Penguin still believes in publishing the best books for everybody to enjoy. We still believe that good design costs no more than bad design, and we still believe that quality books published passionately and responsibly make the world a better place.

So wherever you see the little bird – whether it's on a piece of prize-winning literary fiction or a celebrity autobiography, political tour de force or historical masterpiece, a serial-killer thriller, reference book, world classic or a piece of pure escapism – you can bet that it represents the very best that the genre has to offer.

Whatever you like to read – trust Penguin.